Penguin Book 2719
Meet My Maker The Mad Molecule

J. P. Donleavy was born in New York City in
1926 and educated there and at Trinity
College, Dublin. In addition to *Meet My
Maker The Mad Molecule*, his works include
two novels, *A Singular Man* (in Penguins),
and *The Ginger Man*; a novella, *The Saddest
Summer of Samuel S*; and four plays, *The
Ginger Man*, *Fairy Tales of New York*, *A
Singular Man* and *The Saddest Summer* of
Samuel S.

J. P. Donleavy

Meet My Maker
The Mad Molecule

Penguin Books

Penguin Books Ltd, Harmondsworth,
Middlesex, England
Penguin Books Australia Ltd, Ringwood,
Victoria, Australia

First published in the U.S.A. 1964
Published in Great Britain by The Bodley Head 1965
Published in Penguin Books 1967

Magazines in which material originally appeared
are: *Atlantic Monthly, Esquire, Envoy*, the
Manchester Guardian, Holiday, Lilliput, the *New
Yorker, Playboy, Punch, Queen, Vogue*.
The author wishes to thank the publishers of these
magazines for permission to reprint his stories
in book form

Made and printed in Great Britain by
Hazell Watson & Viney Ltd
Aylesbury, Bucks
Set in Linotype Georgian

Contents

The Romantic Life of Alphonse A

He had an athletic build and walked legs slightly parted like a cowboy. His white haired father had been a pillar of the community, sometimes carrying a small automatic for which he had a license. Alphonse was his one problem child in four. And Alphonse went through life saying often, I want to settle down, you know, have a work out once in a while, keep in good condition, get plenty of sleep, maybe spend a few months in Vermont hunting.

Alphonse had a beautiful way of putting out his hand to say hello. And it went whispered he's nice, isn't he. But long before Alphonse's father died, he said to his son, your life is immoral. Alphonse standing on the carpet of his father's study, his charm hand out, saying, just prove one thing dad, that's all I'm asking, one thing where you know without a doubt I've been immoral.

And Alphonse's father, turning a pencil in thin fingers behind his desk, said 'What about all the speeding fines I've had to pay for you, it was lucky they didn't get you on a drunk charge, what were you doing with perfume all over you.' Alphonse in spring seersucker, scuffing one buckskin shoe with the sole of the other, 'Look Dad, they would have got me on a drunk charge but I put Lila's perfume over me so they couldn't smell it.'

'You flaunt the law.'

'Dad everyone flaunts the law.'

'That's no excuse for a son of mine.'

These meetings mostly monthly had happened right through college. In the same book lined professional room and concluded as Alphonse turned to the door with his father's last words, 'I've got a reputation to uphold in this community.'

On the Autumn days in the stadium exploding with red blue gold, booming bands and yelling young men and women, Alphonse's father, in racoon on the fifty yard line, elbowing his neighbour in the ribs as Alphonse dazzled his way down the field, shouting in the roar, 'That's my boy.' And later in the locker room, Alphonse silent with his sheepish sadness, listened as his Dad said 'I didn't like the way you sized up a few of those plays, you were lucky to win.'

Alphonse with large hands which he laid on his knees, spreading peaceful lonely fingers. And when the four Autumns were over he left behind a string of golden touchdowns with a record of straight A's and on distant tree shaded campuses, three girls heartbroken. In company he greeted new faces easily, asking after their first names and their hobbies like a beer salesman. He brought girls home on weekends who said they loved his family and the way they lived. Mirabelle the maid of twenty years dedicated service presented meals and Sunday jokes and snored at nights across the hall from the guest room. Where Alphonse, when the girl was in the warmth and friendliness of his family, went to visit past midnight to whisper urgently, 'Honey, what would my family think of me if you started screaming.'

The girls changed with the weather. His father said, 'When are you going to settle down and get some responsibility. You use this house like a train station. Find yourself a nice girl. This house is not an hotel.' At these times Alphonse would drive down a dingy Cambridge street to Scollay Square and have a few crazy beers, tipping the bartender and buying the house until everyone present thoroughly loved him. They all said, 'You're a good Joe.' Alphonse said, 'Call me Al.'

Decisions in Alphonse's life were dreams to live after the war. In buckskin shoes, broadcloth shirts, and tasteless ties affected for freedom. He loved the Army, where, as he sat over sheets and sheets, sometimes holding his belly in agonies of repressed laughter, chaos, ineptitude, memorandi and a few orders of the day, sneakily issued by himself, mounted more chaos, ineptitude and memorandi. With lofty dignity he picked the egg shell and debris out of the morning scrambled egg, frequently retaining one of the hard-boiled variety for evening peckishness. Outranked by the entire Army he exercised his love of duty and discipline constantly. Standing before this new, nearly almighty father, in regulation uniform resplendent in spit and polish, saluting snappily upon all and any occasion especially those least particular.

When the last shot was fired, Alphonse, one finger caught in the handle of a cup of tea, sat back in his chair at his desk as his fellow Army clerks rushed out under the Virginia sky to yell. Alphonse for his own little celebration went to the wall and carefully weighted the fire axe in his hands as he had done with so many college baseball bats. Trucks roared by, guns boomed, sirens rang, it seemed such a late milky afternoon. And that night being led to the stockade, Alphonse worried about his physical condition, it having taken six axe blows to divide the master sergeant's desk in half. Later taking six phone calls to Washington for his father to effect an honorable discharge.

And as some friends lapsed into marriage, and he settled down to perhaps a siege of bachelorhood, he took beer and chicken, bologna and pizza in the newly wed kitchens as they told him over and over that he should do it. And taking the occasion as a privilege for a rhyme, Alphonse leaned deeply over the porcelain and said, 'Do you rue it.' Sometimes voices were raised and it was said, 'You're not the same Alphonse A we used to know.'

On a middle September day following that summer, bronzed to a berry, skittish and full of not what you're thinking, Alphonse A stood at attention on the stern of the good ship Franconia in ten fathoms and saluted the flag flying over Fort Jay, murmuring hello in his heart to those in clerkship at the U. S. Military Headquarters of the First Army. That lofty skyline of that terrible temptation to go up and be up and stay up, slowly faded to tiny tips above the water and was gone as the gong went for dinner. At Cobh he took a train to Dublin to a lush stout filled year at Trinity College where he happily read the higher philosophies and lived with a family who took him as one of their own. Washing dishes, gathering praties from their tiny back garden, chopping carrots and cabbage in the red brick scullery.

Diedre who sat next to him at logic lectures asked him to picnics on the beach at Killiney and Alphonse came to whisper in her ear that he loved her like a sister. Night times sometimes down on the shadowy Dublin quays, Alphonse found querulous women, hard but hearty, who spent his money but later liked him for himself. And as this last happy year in his life slowly died and left memories of the green grass of the playing fields where in his Harvard sweat suit he pranced and played a mock football with the rugby team and learned to wield a cricket bat with the best, he packed, waved and wept.

Coming back to America on a cargo ship as a cook, broke and humble. Ladling slops over the side to seagulls. Spying a black fish's haunted fins and sleeping desperate and tired at night in his sack, Diedre he left with a promise of passage to the new world and she said last thing of all, 'Don't lie to me. It makes it worse than never seeing you again.' And he said, 'I don't think I'll ever see you again.' And she laid a lash of hand across his jaw for not lying. Alphonse inaudible as he said it is logical to lie. Turning it into a personal poem on the ship.

It is logical
To lie
To women
And they like it.

Diedre was dark haired and blue eyed. And the memory of her lay lightly on all the water between New York and Europe. As his ship put into the greyness and a sweet sour misty air. It was raining quietly on Fort Jay and the skinny fuzz of Staten Island. He was a dreg. Albeit with a fancy education. Passenger liners plowed by, out to sea, perhaps sorrow and some hundred miles away in the evening they would have a get together dance. And looking at this shore, give me your poor and something, your starving, and perhaps something else. And in the haze, my goodness, a shore, the rubber, the gasoline, not to mention the steel and various alloys. But this was no way to look at the United States and shortly following his taxi ride to a central position, Alphonse wired his father.

AT BILTMORE NO MONEY NEED MORE

It was likely that only a few charges of immorality in the study and some remarks, what do you think I am to have done for you what I've done and you turn out to be a bum. Stopping in that tree shaded Boston street, up the steps of this red brick house where he was born and listened to afternoon baseball games. Mothers go through the house and clean up the childhood dust which dances in the sunlight. Mothers just want to hold you. And father is waiting in the study. Alphonse putting one foot in front of the other, looking at the floor and listening.

'What do you think I am.'

'Look Dad.'

'To have reached where I am and have you grow up to be a bum.'

'Dad.'

'A bum. A suite of rooms. Who the hell do you think you are, and throwing a party on my money. My money, let me make that clear. I didn't ask you to be my son. You've been an unwanted liability in my life. Now you're going to tell me you were Phi Beta Kappa and captain of the football team.'

'I'm not saying anything, Dad.'

'And you're intending to live on it for the rest of your life. Ethics. That's what you need.'

'Dad, look, you must've in your spare time swapped your ideals to make a fast buck.'

'How dare you.'

'Dad, it's life.'

'How dare you indeed.'

Between these faint green walls, moroccan bound books everywhere. Rectitude and fortitude, vice and virtue, eyes in the windows all over the neighbourhood. A cinnamon smell of apples cooking.

'Even you Dad, have said times come when some grim decisions have to be made. And maybe someone gets wiped out overnight.'

'How dare you.'

'I'm telling you Dad, surely it's this way.'

'Get out.'

'Dad I know you've swapped your ideals to make a fast buck. But do I hold it against you.'

'Get out of this room and don't come back till you've got manners to speak to your father.'

Alphonse, avoiding rigid go getting collegiates, took a superficially vulgar residence in a basement in Brooklyn. There were nearly two windows on the street peeking up over a rather rancid little garden. Some yards away out of a patch of earth in the pavement grew a cotton ball tree. His two fellow occupants said, 'We believe in live and let live.' Respectively they had come to New York from Iowa and Maine, meeting at the children's sand pit one summer evening at Eighty Third Street and Central Park West. And together in their close friendship they bought two Dalmatian dogs who lived tied in the bathroom in a most unsanitary manner indeed. But for the low rent and the live and let live, Alphonse was terribly tempted to say, 'For Christ's sake.'

But said little at all. Leaving the front of the house in his yellow Ford to drive north through Brooklyn avoiding Brownsville while murmuring a prayer for the Moors on Livonia Avenue. Amid moaning vehicles, one low voltage brain guiding so many horsepower over the East River and past the grey reminder of Bellevue to ease down a concrete ramp, rolling firmly to a stop on this narrow island of opportunity. Which was a tall brick building with an institutional entrance and a wide floor of desks seven stories up. Where he said, 'Hi Gage, how you doing, Tony what's with you, Frank, all O.K.' And sat, spinning round once in this green office chair. And this Gage stopped once hovering and said into a curious middle distance between them, 'I can't understand it, a guy with your qualifications and background, selling beer.' And the answer taking poetic shape in his head.

> I know
> It may sound queer
> I fear
> That I sell
> Beer.

Slipping quietly away to his canvassing area. Back through reddish Brooklyn streets. The loneliness of noon in some dark tavern where Alphonse A would announce in the barroom shade, 'Gentlemen, I would like to buy you all a drink of a brew which speaks for itself.' It was accidental that Alphonse found this beer absolutely marvelous and believed all the good things he said about it, and therefore mostly said, 'Drink up.' Quietly throughout the next two hours sending perhaps seven men home stoned to their unappreciative wives. And slightly squiffed himself, retired to his club to steam out the wheaty distillate, lying amid towels, hearing the depressing murmur of big deals discussed through the steam. And he reflected with genuine sorrow that he was at the very bottom of the ladder if it had any rungs at all.

Fragmentary women came into his life. And one who was a school teacher in Brooklyn. This Rebecca wore frilly lace on shirt fronts to hide a handy bosom and black severe skirts discreetly across her neat behind. She scuffed her way through the Botanic Garden leaves in flat laced up brown shoes, Alphonse parking his saffron Ford on Flatbush Avenue saying, there's a plane tree growing in Prospect Park. And I like your knowledge and I like your hair and I like the way you've passed through your marriageable days so beautifully unmarried. And how you look with books and how nearly all the men pass your beauty by. And leave your magic all to me.

She was entranced. Almost. And that Sunday evening of Rebecca's first weekend in the warmth of his folks', Alphonse was present at attention for the talk with father in the study. As Dad narrowed his eyes, tilted his head, and tapped ash from a cheroot, 'She's the smartest thing you've ever done. Do you deserve her. I wonder. They've all been trollops in the past stacked up against her. That's all I've got to say, except get out of this beer racket and get a position.'

'I'm glad you said that Dad. I've been thinking that.'

'Don't soft soap me.'

'I'm not, I genuinely feel I ought to have a position deserving of Rebecca.'

'Get one.'

'You said it, Dad.'

Sunday like all the other Sundays, a drive out around Cambridge, down Brattle Street, by the desolation of Fresh

Pond, Clay Pit Pond, Spy Pond and desperately on to the Mystic Lakes until she said, 'Can't we go somewhere nice. Instead of all these ponds.' Rebecca was reared by aunts in Staten Island, with her own little seat for years on the ferry. With books gathered up to her chest as she steamed back and forth to the tip of that tall urbs, and sat with her temperate face and copper hair which said to all who looked, I'm serious minded and no pushover.

And weekend followed weekend to Boston, that good old bean town. And they told friends, yes, yes, we're thinking of settling down, yes, white picket fence, yes, I'm in beer, yes, Rebecca will go on teaching, yes, it's all about time. And about this time, Alphonse A when no one was looking, was looking sad stepping down those cruel steps in Brooklyn through dog musty air to throw himself on his bed in his dissipated room, and say up at the remnants of a Victorian ceiling, 'For Christ's sake they're all murdering me.'

With news of nuptials whispered from uncle to aunt and other eye brow raisers, the shackles and chains closed around Alphonse A. He thought of ships and islands, the deep green spring of Dublin where dying is no defeat. And where one must suppose in all honesty, living was no victory. And now driving to friends' houses, pleading over the porcelain, tell me before it's too late, what's it really like, I'm too young to love under contract.

Kisses on her neck as they parked under trees, seeking shelter for his sad hands under her clothes. And she said, 'I will when we wed.' And Alphonse said, 'But we're grown human beings, besides I'm an athlete needy of a normal love relationship.' Rebecca said, 'Tell it to the Marines.' In the silence that followed and in the longer lonelier and later ones, Alphonse's hands wanted to go around her throat. Instead, he drove too fast and it always happened, down some pyjamaed judge's basement, three in the morning, pay thirty dollars, and 'Don't do it again son, shame on you.'

Till that weekend. How she smiled up proudly as voices knew him in the stands as Harvard was soundly trounced by Yale. She climbed up on the crook of his arm cheering hopefully and Alphonse said not a hope. But in the afternoon golden sun it was a large day of old friendships. Sailing into handshakes on a slight collision course. And later they drank beer, sang, and had dinner on a roof just as Fall was chilling the windows closed and the tide was turning in the trees.

They kissed in the garage, hard by the summer screens stacked for storage, and she said, 'I've been happy, Al, happy.' Following in the wake of this sentiment to the third landing where she pecked him goodnight on the cheek and said, 'Thank you for today.' Alphonse saying to himself, don't press the advantage, just keep it warm so it doesn't cool. In his bedroom, lying, listening, and waiting on the pine perfumed sheets.

A quick reconnoiter outside his door for any moving member of the household. Avoid squeaking stairs number four and six. Move on the right floor board of the landing which is securely nailed to the carrying rafter. And beware stairs number two, six and seven. As one counts going up in the dark. And she, perhaps, he hoped, lay lightly in the twilight of a glittering dream of Alphonse, high up, familiar with people you want to know, Rebecca, forever, and say, gee they're my closest friends to whom I could go if I didn't have my subway fare. And today, the game and the way they welcomed Alphonse and how his old coach said so sincerely, 'We could use you in there, today, Al, we really could.'

Alphonse A had a conscience, saying a variety of things. You're real rotten. A little reflected stardom as a hasbeen and you ride roughshod over ethics, devoid of one vestige of moral momentum. Alphonse, a guiding hand pausing on the bannister, taking up his defense. Hush now. This world is a jungle. My moral momentum may be minimum but it is more than most. And one floor board here is a lulu. I'm coming to borrow her toothbrush or something, with maybe a minute to chat about the bristles. Must knock. No excuse for a lack of manners. If I barge in unannounced she might go tearing through the ceiling and roll down the roof outside, loosening all the slates. The risks I take are desperate. If I could behave with this abandon in the business world, The Chase Manhattan Bank would send me greetings on my birthday. With maybe three clerks to sing,

> O Alphonse
> A
> Have a happy
> Birthday.

Rebecca distant in the dark. Copper hair all black on her pillow. Alphonse A, time 3 a.m., attired in dressing gown, approaching from the flank. Deploying and moving forward under cover of knowing every inch of this soft carpet. She sits suddenly bolt upright. Alphonse listening to the deep intake of breath signifying panic and a large piercing scream about to come. But parting his lips and lighting the way ahead with the beacon of his smile. A friendly ship draws near, dear. To an unfriendly voice.

'Who's that.'
'Me.'
'What are you doing here.'
'Just me. Nothing.'
'You are.'
'Not so loud. Would you like an extra pillow.'
'I've got two.'
'Maybe another one.'
'Go.'
'Please. Let me stay.'
'Go.'
'Gee just five minutes.'

'No go.'

'No.'

'I'll scream.'

'Honey what would my family think of me if you started screaming.'

'They'd think you were a sneaking rat.'

'Honey.'

'Go.'

'Just let me slip under the sheets with you for a second. Promise. Just one second. I'm shivering.'

'Go.'

'But I mean we've been going together for weeks. Don't you have any mercy. A little connubial hors d'oeuvre.'

'Not until you marry me.'

'Honey you'll have the nuptials, any time now.'

'Ha. Ha. Ha.'

'Rebecca, can't you see I'm desperate. Five minutes solace. I'm lonely and forlorn. Can't you understand. Let me in. The bed.'

'Not before nuptials.'

The struggle began routinely enough. An arm lock using the Jap reversible grip on the wrist. The knee cover to stop the leg flail. And some tiny soothing words whispered lightly from time to time, there, there, easy. As one of her hands escapes from the Jap lock to send the bedside lamp crashing to the floor. It is always hard to believe in these moments that they mean it, so many times they say months later, I wanted you to, if only you had gone on fighting. Tonight Alphonse was fighting. And bedclothes are on the floor along with the lamp. Not even time in this frantic festivity to hear if Mirabelle is still snoring across the hall.

'Let me go, you brute.'

'Rebecca, please be civilised.'

The light was a pale pale yellow and it flooded gently in from the hall. Crossing the crumpled white coverlet with a frail shadow. The frosted broken shell of glass. A breeze banging the white wooden anchor of the Venetian blind. High up a plane comes over Cambridge to cross the Charles River and fly in low over Boston Harbor to land. A cardboard cylinder of salt, a picture of a little girl with a yellow umbrella walking in the rain on blue. Tender moments when you were doing nothing at all, at all, some tiny piece of childhood faintly tells as it comes back to mind, that some things will never happen again. Until they happen.

Alphonse's father spoke with a sad sincerity. A thin bony man in the doorway. Patrician perhaps, two long white hands holding the cord of his robe. Pillar of the neighborhood. His lips moving a few times, collecting a low threadbare silence around his words.

'I will give you ten minutes to get out of this house forever.'

Dawn in the street as Alphonse tucked his possessions in the car. Huffing over a wicker hamper of books. One can rupture in the most fraught of times. A portable radio bought in an Army PX, a quiet little plan for a supply of music after the war. The box of sweat socks, bow ties and random haberdashery. Some big shouldered jackets for off field wear to look like a football star. One class picture to memorise each face in order to get out of the way when it's seen coming along Madison Avenue. And with this unromantic antique aggregate of property, Alphonse A set off down Beacon Street on a straight line southerly out of Boston town.

New York that winter, terrible biting winds down grey canyons. And one dismal day he moved from Brooklyn across the river to Manhattan Island. Making wet tracks in a slush which lay on the flat friendless wasteland he left behind. Harry his beer boss said, 'Al, wouldn't you be happier maybe, let me fix you up with a territory in the Eastern Bronx.' And with a little map tacked to the green wall of his new apartment, Alphonse planned out a campaign using military references he remembered from his first seventy two hours in the Army and had never had cause to use again. At night he cooked in his kitchenette on an electric grill which frequently threw him against the wall with shocks.

Rebecca became a faint figure, her own little seat now, he guessed, on the Sixty Ninth Street ferry back and forth to Brooklyn. Hoping still for some nibble before nuptial he'd taken her for drinks to a group of friends, who sat sporty in big deep chairs and never once spoke to her the whole evening. As joss sticks smoked and canapes sailed into mouths. They asked him, 'Hey, Al, we hear the old man kicked you out on your rear, no free loading in bean town no more.' And with head thrown back Alphonse laughed until putting his hand over his lips when Rebecca rushed from the room.

The ride that night out to Staten Island, Rebecca carped. He took breathers round the outside deck of the ferry. She said, 'The cheap common company you keep.' And the journey back across the Narrows, little waves as the currents of black water met off Fort Jay. A barge was alight in the thick mist and Alphonse went forward to stand bow front staring ahead at the dim beads of windows strung up and down in the distance. He had a solitary hot dog and coffee and quietly listened as a seated odd ball citizen numbled, 'We need more funeral parlors in Richmond County.'

Nights Alphonse slept as sound as a bell, ringing only when it was time to rise. To go forth across the luminous land of the East Bronx. First standing at the ice box door, draped in an undergarment defying description, legs crossed in a pose of thought, eating a slice of pineapple and pecan coffee cake. And Harry, his unurgent sad eyed superior, who quietly felt Alphonse was a great guy if he would only get out there and canvass. And was pleased when one day Alphonse came into his glass cage in the corner of their office floor and said, 'Mr G, let it not be gainsaid that I want to sell more beer in the Bronx.'

Alphonse in the resolute weeks that followed, made his lonely pioneering way along Two Hundred and Thirty Third Street and further east. Breaking all sales records through Hunt's Point, Clason's Point and Throg's Neck. Only once, in a side road parked under a tree near a vacant lot with kids playing in the clouds of dust, did Alphonse crack like a soft boiled egg. Letting the tears come down as he looked at his knees shining under the crease he'd made with his own iron that morning. His head slumped on his chest, wiping the salt water away with the back of his hand. A police patrol car went by and they looked.

But in this new demeanour, Alphonse spread good will, shooting out a hand leading with his right shoulder, he grinned and squeezed his economic way upward. Always a glad word for the man who was slowing in endeavor, whose goose might be slowly cooking. He asked after people's families. After their cats and dogs with nary a qualm for the Dalmatians that might be among them. He led groups from one soirée to another, saying, 'Let's go, gang, it's hard but it's fair, but gang, let's go.' At traffic lights as they turned to green, he said again back into his crowded car, 'Go. Go.' And old friends said, 'This is the Alphonse A we used to know.'

Ashamed of his recent dwellings, Alphonse moved again. To the East Sixties, and lived behind three bow fronted windows three stories up. Entering from the street on black and white tile steps, between boxwood shrubs and through heavy filigree steel on frosted glass. An Eastern Embassy across the street, a black suited member of whose staff waited discreetly each morning while a leashed black poodle lifted a leg on a newly planted tree. In these new digs which he tried to keep secret, Alphonse spent Wednesday evenings polishing Victorian weighing instruments of which he had collected three.

Until this one Wednesday when early afternoon he'd returned from the reaches of Westchester Heights along the Boston Post Road slightly feeling in the dumps. By appointment he'd paid a solitary visit to the Bronx Annex of the American Indian, wishing they had never given up to the newcomers. And as the day ended Alphonse took bun and Coca Cola at a table on the terrace of Central Park Zoo. Kids' blue, red and yellow balloons caught up in the trees. Those slow of wit went lurking and matching theirs at the other animals behind the bars. The sun blinding red in the windows high up over Fifth Avenue. Bees hummed distinctly in the ivy and cheerless growls came from the big cats. All drowned by the screams of a little kid whacked by his father across the arse.

And Alphonse A slowly walked back to his address, looking up between grey stone fronted buildings at the sky. His decision to make money just in case it brought happiness. And to avoid marriage in case it brought chains. And turning into his entrance he rose standing over the orange and blue mosaic of an eagle on the elevator floor. A pale yellow envelope lay next to his evening newspaper on the marble table outside his door. Alphonse said to himself, someone's dying or someone's dead.

FATHER SERIOUSLY ILL COME IMMEDIATELY

That night he took the last train to Boston. A lonely figure crossing the deserted pink floor of Grand Central, the Zodiac spread on the ceiling in blue, gold and studded with electric stars. With a magazine opened vacantly on his lap, the train moved out between the dark pillars dripping rain from the street above. Coming up between the red brick tenements when you look down on the dark pavements and see things you saw before. A funeral chapel, freshly baked pizza 10¢ a slice, superior shoe hospital and suddenly, lit by a flash of lightning, large black letters on a high grey wall.

A bright moon in the cool night over Boston. Alphonse A lugging his catch all made from an Irish horse to a taxi in front of South Station. Taking this vehicle through all the tight familiar turnings of nearly a year ago. House with dim lights lit and a glow from behind the relic shades of his father's front bedroom. And from the roadway looking up across this summer darkness, a feeling of Christmas. Holly, mistletoe, when you cry and cry as a little boy knowing what Ma and Pa are giving for a present, because sneak and betrayer, you spied under the day bed in the sewing room.

Alphonse with a looselimbed gait up the steps. The door opening before he could knock. His small mother holding her big son tightly. The hall stand chockablock with canes and one shillelagh. A ne'er do well uncle standing near the open door of his father's library. His dark haired sister, college graduated, coming down the stairs already dressed in black and tears streaming down her face. Hello to Radcliffe girls everywhere. And Mirabelle making the biggest racket of all, appearing everywhere with moans, an empty tray and face. While his brother sat over a book in the kitchen studying for an exam.

Tonight he thought the trip was a false alarm, just one of those crazy or not so crazy things families do to get back together again. And his mother said, 'Would you like to go up.' And the thing you think you will never do but do. Up the steps, stairs number three, eight and nine and the board on the landing outside his father's door which ought to have squealed loudly one night in the past.

The doctor comes out of the room. One of his father's oldest friends, whose eyes were full of secrets and who Autumns ago basted venison in the basement kitchen after a hunting trip and with his father in their cups might, just for the devil, sing as a barbershop quartet.

'Hi Doc.'

'Hi Alphonse, he's asleep, only stay a minute, I don't know how long he's got.'

The door ajar. All yellow light. A bedside lamp is glowing. A tray of whiteness and white things. Like a little baby between the sheets. Who needs a mother. And kicked his big athletic son out of the house with thirteen final words and now lies without the strength of signature left.

In these quiet seconds as Alphonse stood over the bed, he knew his father was at that moment dying, quietly choking on his own breath. As he stepped closer, he felt just below his eyes across the soft part of his jaw his muscles making him smile and grin. And the beer salesman in him trying to stop it. And he couldn't, standing on the soft carpet, grinning from ear to ear.

His father's funeral was for the last time down the tree shaded street with its new leaves. Across two highways and train tracks. Great black iron gates. Gloved attendants in their quiet grey uniforms. All the trees and white sepulchres on the side of the hill. A magnolia fluffing its gentle flowers out, all pink against the stiff silver birch and tall elms older than all the graves.

The Mad Molecule

I woke on that terrible day and mixed the shredded apple in my raw porridge oats and poured on the cream. I know what's good for me. I put on the shoes with the golfer's soles, walked silently down the stairs and out into a great blue sky and along the river's warm sweet smell.

Two days ago I looked down through my sparkling microscope. Opened up the diaphragm for more light and there it was. I said my my, what's this, it moves. Bumping pinpoint bouncing merrily, wow, did a standing broad jump of ten microns just then. This is most extraordinary.

I didn't think I'd tell the others but I had to. Great believer in the professional courtesy. Crowding round they said it was some crystalline salt. How could they be so cruel. I told them go away. I gave it the test for proteins. It passed.

At lunch I went with my little bag of garlic bread, which for various reasons I must eat alone, to the little churchyard that juts out a soft green silence in the river. I watched the gasworks making gas hiding all the heaven and the tiny derricks scooping coal. I let my sad grey face smile at the excursion boats waving by. And sunk my teeth into the crackling crust while the little toy train went tootling over the bridge. And as I looked up river to more smoke mountains wearing lightning conductors like a crown, I said hello in my heart to neglected people everywhere.

I went back through the streets of tired houses tight between the raging factories. All their windows trimmed in green with curtains gold and closed. To discover something is such great joy. A new molecule, a whole new series which

I may call the mad proteins. And buy one of these little houses, rest a retired heart in there, slippered feet up and lungs wheezing while night goes by. And perhaps in an attic recess with slides and books quietly dipping my oil immersion lens. I don't want much.

And there on my table the little white memo near my curling vines. Mr So and so wants to see Mr D. I looked around at my professional colleagues. All their faces turned away, huddled with guilt. As soon as my back is turned. This is what I get for courtesy.

Along this wide corridor and up the fireproof stairs. See a tug out there. If only I could be a captain of one of those little ships, just ply my way back and forth, smiling from shore to shore. Where there's no one to betray me over a molecule.

Knocking on this glass door. Come in. Mr D, do please sit down. I prefer to stand. Very well, Mr D, but what I have got to say may be difficult, if you follow me. I am following. Now, Mr D, have you been feeling all right recently. I'm feeling very well. No headaches? Sir, do make yourself clear. Mr D, as you know, you've been with us for nearly a year and we understand you've done some interesting if rather obscure work, however, we feel you need a rest, somewhere quiet perhaps, the ships' whistles are nerve racking at times. Sir, I love them. That may be, Mr D, however, it is the considered opinion of this department that you need a rest. I'm not tired. I understand that, Mr D, but even so it is our policy to give people a great deal of latitude and even longitude when feasible, but we feel you need a rest and in your own interests to go the south of somewhere for a month, naturally at our expense. Although I like you, Mr D, we don't feel you ought to return here. I am sorry, Mr D.

I was sorry, too. Mr So and so offered his hand. Success had given him a warm friendly smile. So sadly I collected my little vines I let grow on my bench and looked my last look from my window. I walked away with the rich gleaming joy of my mad molecule.

I bought some flowers, red and white carnations, at the barrow. I went across the bridge. And back to my little room up the stairs. I put the mad molecule under my own microscope, focused and then it jumped a mile. I was so pleased. I thought I had been seeing things.

At Longitude and Latitude

They thought I was crazy when I bought the island. I said it was a bargain. And got one of these unsinkable rubber rafts. They asked me was I worried about sharks. What a laugh. I said what are you blind? Can't you see I've got this new type harpoon? Any of these sharks come near me, he gets it right between the eyes.

Then they said I'd starve. So I told them about the deep freeze with mutton, chops and beef. I could even freeze soup. And just in case, I had my handbook for survival that tells you about chewing bark.

So on an afternoon in June I set sail. They were all there on the dock watching me. Wise guys making cracks about wait till the hurricane. I know the type, just trying to get the wind up me. So I waved the weather report right in their faces. I said read this, it says clear sailing and besides maybe you're just jealous because I'm going to be nice and lonely for a couple of months listening to my portable gramophone. I think, deep inside me, I hated them all anyway. All the kind of guys who lob balls into the sun when you're playing tennis.

The sky was bright and clear blue, the outboard motor purring away. It was twenty two miles. In maybe three hours with a good current, I'll be able to see the little hill with the palm trees and where I fixed the flag pole. That was another thing they were beefing about, they thought it was anarchy to fly my own personal flag and that the coast guard would think it was distress or something. When it was only me.

About three thirty there was a slight westerly breeze and a few clouds. I thought just a touch of right rudder. A few of them said they would come out late this afternoon in Harold's cruiser just to see if maybe I sprung a leak and had to use the rubber raft. They won't leave me alone. But there's no sign of anybody. And there's no other island like mine anywhere in these parts. Somehow they just don't want to see a guy go off to be by himself. Always have to make out he's a jerk or his politics want to be watched.

I figure I ought to be coming in sight any minute now, although it's taking longer than I expected. And when you're out here all alone you get ideas. Maybe a little left rudder. I can't wait to get up a good charcoal fire and singe up a nice thick steak. I always say, a few hours at sea brings on an appetite.

When I bought it I thought the guy was asking too much but he said he'd throw in the boat as well as the diesel generator and enough oil to last a year. He told me he wasn't the introspective type although you sure could do some serious thinking on that island and the fishing was great. So I thought with electricity, water converter and shower, what more could I want except to get away from Harold and the others for a few months. And Harold's wife made that nasty remark that I didn't know any of them anymore since I took the speech improvement course. There's nothing wrong with making sure you're never misunderstood and I think being able to communicate ideas clearly ought to be uppermost in anybody's mind.

The way I figure I ought to be there by now. Maybe it's just this slight overcast. I feel like a shower and shave and then a nice can of beer in the hammock and tune into shore for some dance music. And I'll put out the string of colored lights tonight. Wonderful how they give you that festive feeling.

I think more left rudder. Might have miscalculated this current. This sea is some size. I'm just a needle in a haystack

29

out here. At the beach picnic Myrtle showed she just couldn't take it, getting sore when I slipped the fish down her back. Must be sorry now she called me a boor. She'd probably like to come stay on the island but I'm inviting none of them.

Maybe I better try right rudder. Not a sign of shore anywhere. And it's getting dark. This calls for checking position. My God. I'm here. It's gone.

Call Me Cheetah

Our host, this tall friendly man, brought us through his kitchen to the garage to pick out a car to take us home. I said I would like blue. And we went off down the parkway at 3 a.m. through the scratchy trees. We talked of service, armies and navies. One said he had to go in the draft soon and another had been. He said he got in a band and played the piano and that it was all right. Jack said it was the indignity of it.

There was some snow in tiny piles along the road and the north sides of trees. And I said in the Navy I was a tough man to get to work. And told them how they lined up ten thousand men every morning, me among them, to read off the names and then compress them all together, slicing sections off the ends for working parties. And they never got me. They kept us out in the open but I would leap out of this dark gathering with all their white hats and streak away to get lost between the quonset huts with them after me, dozens of them. I loved it. And they were waiting for me to do it with extra guards posted everywhere to stop me from getting away. A cheer went up from the ranks when I struck out for liberty or library for the lazy morning behind the magazine. I could hear them yelling get that wise guy and from the big brass boss man with the microphone up there screaming quite crazily, by God stop him, stop him, get that man, get him. There is an animal. Called a cheetah. I ran streamlined against the wind. Naturally I practiced every day. At times I was aghast at my nerve but my little heart was tempted by applause. It got so that these ten thousand men would wait in miraculous silence for me to make my break and I think the boss man was getting worried about the prestige of the service at stake or get me and make an example. I think he yelled once that I'll see you get ten years if it's the last thing I do. This latter quite understandably made me think and of course travel faster.

And that one and last morning when they almost got me. Several jeeps were ordered on the scene, brimming with these brutes. Distasteful types brave with clubs. I was careful to look for lethal weapons. Roll call was taken and then the sections pushed together. I waited looking up into this Virginia sky all cold, rolling out to sea over this silence and no peep from anyone. I've got to do it, please don't let them get me. My brains and feet against their clubs and wheels. I can't help savouring it and there they are ready on all sides. They knew the general section of the crowd I would leap from but they weren't taking any chances, cars patrolling up and down, eagle eyes on every face and people shining innocence back. Me too. But after my usual pause for the tension that's in it, I began to get sceptical, a jeep had stopped right in front of me. For a second I thought they might know it was me but one of the men pointed to a chap up a bit and said watch that jerk there it looks like him.

I put my collar up a little higher and got my cap down. Half a minute went by and smiles appearing on guards' faces. That was it. I was off. I ran straight at them. Whoa. Those clubs raised up in the sky, this means detour for sure. A massive fantastic cheer went up and another as I swerved up the road executing my first dodge. As they were getting out of the jeep the driver started off and three guards were thrown to the ground, thank God. There was a laugh. The officer in charge was screaming such gibberish that I almost stopped to listen.

I made for the huts weaving my way away. Feet behind me and then a guard stepped out in front, wow, they were in earnest. This guard managed to say his last words first.

I got him with his own club. But he slowed me down and I had only one hope left. Bizarre deception. I ran into a hut and out the other end to shake them off and quickly into another, taking off my coat and jumper, hat too, and proceeded out the other end casually, suppressing the breath to walk over to a washstand and plunge my garments into the water.

As I stood there busily scrubbing this man came puffing around the corner. He stopped, looked at me. I said to him, say you guys still after that crazy fool? He said something quite obscene to me.

A Fairy Tale of New York

Three o'clock in February. All the sky was blue and high. Banners and bunting and people bunched up between. Greetings and sadness.

Great black box up from the deep hold, swinging in the air high over the side of the ship. Some of the stevedores taking off their caps and hoods. With quiet whisperings, swiveling it softly on a trolley and pushing it into a shed.

Cornelius Christian standing under the letter C. The customs man comes over.

'I'm sorry sir about this. I know it isn't a time you want to be annoyed by a lot of questions but if you could just come with me over to the office I'll try to get this over as quickly as possible. It's just a formality.'

Walking across the pier through the rumbling carts, perfumes, furs and tweeds, the clanging chains, and into the little warm hut with type writers pecking. Tall dark customs man, his fist with a pencil on a piece of paper.

'I understand this happened aboard ship.'

'Yes.'

'And you're an American and your wife was foreign.'

'Yes.'

'And you intend burial here.'

'Yes.'

'It's just that we've got to make sure of these things because it can save a lot of trouble later. Don't want to burden you with anything unnecessary. Do you have any children travelling.'

'Just my wife and myself.'

34

'I understand. And are all your other possessions your own property, all personal effects. No fine art, antiques. Your're not importing anything.'

'No.'

'Just sign here. Won't be anything else and if you have any trouble at all don't hesitate to get in touch with me right away. Here's my name and I'll straighten out any difficulty. Just Steve Kelly, customs'll get me. Vine funeral home phoned here just a while ago. I told him everything was all right and he says you can go see them at their office, or phone any time this afternoon or tonight. You take it easy.'

'Thanks very much.'

Customs man giving Christian a pat on the back.

'And say, Mr Christian, see the stevedore, guy with the fur jacket. Just tell him Steve said you'd help me with my stuff. O.K. Don't worry about anything.'

'Thanks.'

Out through the grinding winches, clicking high heels, the stacks of gay baggage and colored labels. The great tall side of ship. And coming out to it as it sat on the sea in Cork Harbor. A stiff cold vessel. All of us bundled up as the tender tugged us out on the choppy water. And left the pink houses on the shore twirling early morning turf smoke in the sky. Black rivets on the ship's side. And I climbed up behind her. On the stairway swaying over the water. And now through this jumble and people gathering each other in their arms. This stevedore with fur jacket, a hook tucked under his arm. Hard muscles across his jaw.

'Excuse me, Steve said you'd help me with my stuff.'

'Oh yeah, sure. Sure thing. Got much.'

'Three small trunks, two bags.'

'O.K. You just follow me all the way. I'll put the stuff down the escalator. Meet me the bottom of the stairs. You want a taxi.'

'Please.'

Under the roof of girders and signs. No tipping. Escalator rumbling down with trunks and crates. Crashing and crushing. The treatment they give things would break open her box. And they shout, This way folks. Five bucks, Grand Central. Three fifty, Penn Station. The stevedore has scars on his face, keeps his hands on his hips. 'Mr Christian, this guy will take you wherever you want to go. Stuff's on.'

'Here.'

'No no. I don't want any money. I don't take money for a favor. You'll do the same for somebody. That way it goes round the world.'

'Thanks.'

'Forget it.'

Cornelius Christian opening the door into this gleaming cab. Horns honk everywhere. This driver with a green cap turns around.

'Where to, bud.'

'I don't know. Have to think of somewhere.'

'Look, I haven't got all day. I want to catch another boat coming in.'

'Do you know where I can get a room.'

'I'm no directory bud.'

'Anything.'

'Place is full of hotels.'

'Do you know anywhere I can get a room.'

'Boardinghouse for a guy like you. Just sort of dumps I know. This is some time to start looking. Everybody wants me to find a room I'd be starving. As it is I make peanuts. O.K. I know a place West Side near the museum.'

Taxi twisting away. With smiles and arms laden with coats others get into cabs. The trip is over. Some made friends. And we go up a hill to the roaring highway.

'It's none of my business but what's a guy like you doing coming all the way over here with nowhere to go. You don't sound like a guy got no friends, don't look it neither. O.K. Takes all sorts of people to make a world. Keep tell-

36

ing my wife that, she doesn't believe me. Thinks everybody's like her. Across there long.'

'Went to college.'

'Good education over there. Don't you feel lonely.'

'No, don't mind being alone.'

'That right. Got a right to feel that way if you want. But look at this, how can you feel alone. Everything looking like it's going to explode. And I got a face looks like a monkey. Know why. Because I used to own a pet shop till a relative got the big idea to make a lot of money. So what happens, I lose the whole thing. Now I'm driving a hack. Kick in your teeth and every guy after a fast buck. What a life. Keep going, keep going till you can't stop.'

Christian folding white gloved hands in his lap. Cars stream along the highway. The wail of a police car zooming by.

'Look at that, some guy murdered his mother for a dime. Guy like me got to drink milk all day, live like a baby. I tell you, it's a crime. Sweat our guts out. Something awful. Goddam place jammed with foreigners. Think they'd stay in Europe instead of coming over here and crowding us out. You foreign.'

'No.'

'You could pass for foreign. It's O.K. with me mister if you're foreign. My mother came from Minsk.'

Clouds come grey and east. Ice down there on the edge of the river. Smoky red weak sun.

Taxi turns down off the highway. Between the pillars holding up the street above. Serve beer in there. Bar stools and sawdust. Stevedores with hooks. They say keep your mouth shut and you won't get hurt. Safe in a crowd. Close in there by the elbows, next to the sleeves where all around me are just hands to shake and squeeze.

'O.K. mister here we are. Give me five bucks.'

Red grey stone. An iron fence. Where the rich lived years ago. Tall steps up. First five dollars gone.

'Mister ring the bell downstairs and I'll take your bags, never get rich this way but you look lonely. Mrs Grotz'll take care of you. She's crazy, but who isn't.'

Mrs Grotz, cross eyed, wrapped in a black coat and a collar of silver fox, standing in the door.

'What's your business mister.'

'He's all right, Ma, just back from college over in Europe. Just ain't got no friends.'

'Everyone ought to have friends.'

'How do you know he wants them.'

'Friendship means a lot, you crazy cab driver.'

'My wife thinks I'm crazy too, but my kids think I'm God.'

'Go home you crazy cab driver. Follow me mister, I got a nice room.'

Carrying the bags behind this large bottom shifting up the stairs. In the onion smell. And scent of dust.

'Stairs for me is work mister. Got to do everything myself. Since my husband. He drop dead right in his underwear. Right while I was watching. Such a shock. Go to turn off the lamp and drop dead right on his face. I'm nervous and shaking like this ever since. So all husbands drop dead sometime. You think they have manners and do it quiet in the hospital.'

A room with red curtains high on the windows. Double bed like one I saw in Virginia where once I was walking down a street and climbed in a train standing in the hot sun. Always wishing I could save the heat for the winter.

'Four fifty dollars a night or twenty dollars a week. Look what I supply, radio, shelves, gas stove, hot water. Don't play the radio loud.'

'Could I let you know in a day or two how long I'll be staying.'

'Give you till Friday and you got to make up your mind. You got a funny voice, you English. Learn to speak at college.'

'Just a bit.'

'Was that accent you was born with.'

'I don't know.'

'Give me four dollars and fifty cents.'

New world. Opening up the suitcases on the bed. Turn on the oven. Out into the hall past another brown door. Everything in the dark. And cars go by in the street like boats and soft bubbles.

Find the switch for the light in this bathroom. Green towel crumpled on the floor. Lift the seat. All gentlemen are requested. When little you never lift the seat and mommy tell you lift the seat. Pick up the towel. Go back. This door has a name on it under the cellophane. And now the only thing I can do is wait and wait and wait. It's got to go away. She could never pack things and her bag's a mess. I told her she was sloppy, why don't you fold things up. And I've got to go down there. To a funeral parlor. Come all the way here to a funeral parlor. Just wash my face. No one to be with her. And I was so full of dying myself. I hope I know how to get down there after all these years. How much is it going to cost. Just end up being buried among a lot of strangers.

Christian steps down into the street. Grey tweed on his back. White gloves on hands. Street full of shadows. And dark cars parked. And straight ahead the stale stiff fingers of trees. After so much ocean. And I don't know what to say to this man. He'll be in black or something. Do I have to give him a tip or a cigar. He might think I'm not sorry enough and can't concentrate on the death.

Grey tall windows of the museum. Down these steps to the subway. Chewing gum everywhere. Turnstile reminds me of horses. Coin goes in so neatly. Click through. Could step right under a train. Just let it roar right over me. What have you got to touch to get electrocuted. How would they know to take me and put me with Helen. It would have to be written down in my wallet. In case of death take me to the Vine funeral home and bury me with Helen. So slaughtered you could put me round her in the same casket. I just can't bear for you to be cold and you said last thing of all to put you in the ground. And you always wore a green shadow around your eyes. Came near me in your silk rustling dress you sounded hollow inside. Listening with your eyes. And the first day at sea I didn't want to see you spend the two dollars for a deck chair. Now I'd let you have it. I'd let you have anything now. Helen, you could have got two deck chairs or three and I'd have said nothing. It wasn't the money, I didn't want you to get cold because you looked so ill you'd freeze up there and no one knew how sick you were. And I pulled on the towel. Pulled it right out of your hands when you said you'd spend the two dollars. It wasn't the money, I'd tear up two dollars here right on this platform. God, it was the money. I've lost you.

Head bowed. A white knuckle rubbing under an eye. A man steps near.

'Are you all right, buddy.'

'Yes I'm all right. Just a lot of dust blown up in my eyes.'

'O.K., buddy, just wanted to make sure.'

Roaring train in the tunnel. Sweeping into the station. Train with the tickling noise under the floor. Doors growl shut. Then up, out, crossing each avenue, when the lights turn red and the cars slide up and stop. And it's all so new around me and so old. When I was young and walking here I heard a car screech and hit a boy. Saw the white shirt on his shoulder. And I wondered if all the people would be gathering around and keep him warm and not like me running away.

Where the street slants down, further on, tall buildings and a river. Closer. There it is. Double curtained doors, two evergreens on either side. Push through. God, what a place for you. Soft carpeted hall, luxurious in here. Warm green light flowing up the walls. So soft everything. This isn't bad. This door's open. It gleams and I'll knock. Man's black shoes and gartered black socks sticking out from a desk. They move and shine. His hand in front of me.

'Good evening, you're Mr Christian aren't you.'

'Yes.'

'I'm sorry that you've had to come. I'm Mr Vine, please sit down.'

'Thank you.'

'Will you smoke. Cigarette. Cigar.'

'No thanks.'

'Go ahead, make yourself comfortable. There are only a few little things here. Customs man who dealt with you telephoned after you left the pier. Very nice of him and I'll certainly do everything I can Mr Christian. Only these to sign.'

'Thanks.'

'I'm not just an ordinary man in this business. It means a great deal to me and if there is any special help I can give anyone I'm really glad to do it. So understand that.'

'That's nice of you.'

'We can only do our best Mr Christian. We try to understand sorrow. I've arranged burial at Greenlawn. Do you know New York.'

'Yes, I was born here.'

'Then you may know Greenlawn. One of the most beautiful cemeteries in the world and it's always a pleasure to visit. My wife's buried there as well and I know it's a place of great peace. We realise sorrow Mr Christian. I'll take care of all the immediate details for you and you can have a chat with them later on. All under my personal direction. Arranged as soon as you wish.'

'Could it be arranged for tomorrow morning.'

'Yes. Will it give mourners time. The notice will only be in tomorrow's Daily News, only give anybody couple of hours to get here.'

'I'll be the only mourner.'

'I see.'

'No one knew we were coming to New York.'

'I can put you in our small suite there across the hall.'

'Just for a few minutes. I want to keep it very short.'

'I understand. In the way of flowers.'

'I'd like something simple. Perhaps a wreath with My Helen.'

'Of course. Something simple. I'll see to it myself. We try to make friends with sorrow Mr Christian. That way we come to know it. You'd like us to use glass. For permanence.'

'That's all right.'

'And where are you located.'

'Near the Museum of Natural History.'

'I'm pleased you're near there. There's much to reflect upon in that building. We'll send our car for you.'

'Is that anything extra.'

'Included Mr Christian. Shall I make it nine thirty, ten, whenever you wish.'

'Nine thirty is fine.'

'Mr Christian, would you like now to have a little drink before you go. Some Scotch.'

'Well I would. Are you Irish, Mr Vine.'

'My mother was. My father was German.'

Mr Vine's little snap of the head and blink of the eyes, crossing his soft canary carpet. Puts a neat white hand under an illuminated picture. Sunlight filtering through mountain pines and brass name beneath says In The Winter Sun. Panels drawing apart. Shelves of bottles, glasses, and the small white door of a refrigerator. He must drink like a fish. Pick him up like a corpse every night.

'Soda, Mr Christian.'

'Please.'

'Now, the way you said that. Just one word. I can tell by your voice that you're an educated man Mr Christian. I also like your name. I never had very much in the way of

42

education. I was a wildcatter in Texas and then became the manager of an oil field. Wouldn't think of it to look at me, would you. I left school when I was nine years old. I've always wanted to be in this business but I was thirty before I got a chance to do a high school course. Did it in the Navy, then went to morticians' school when I came out. It makes you feel closer to people. It's dignified. And art. When you see what you can do for someone who comes to you help- less. To recreate them just as they were in life. Makes you able to soften things. You're a man I can talk to, a person who's got a proper mental attitude. I can always tell. There are some of them who make you sick. Only thing I don't like about the business are the phonies and I get my share of them. Here, have another, do you good.'

'Thanks.'

'Some people think I'm outspoken but I've given a lot of satisfaction and people put their whole families in my hands, even in a big city like this. I opened up another branch in the West Fifties. But I like it best here where I began. My two little girls are growing up into big women now. You meet people from all walks of life. I'm a bit of a philosopher and I feel anything you've got to learn you'll learn just through what you have to do with people, in that way I never miss an education. It's a fact, I never graduated. It's especially sad when I bury those who did. But every- thing is how a person conducts themselves. That's how I know all about you, customs man said over the phone you were a real gentleman. Would you like now for me to show you the establishment. If you don't it's all right.'

'I don't mind.'

'You'd like to feel that she was somewhere where she's really at home. Come along, we're empty now, there's just two at my other branch although it's a busy time of the year.'

Mr Vine rising. Gently bent forward. Flicks his head and bends one shoulder up to his ear. Frown around his eyes and hair sticks straight up on his head. Holding door ajar. Smiling with his tilted face.

'I never want to have an establishment of mine get so big you lose the personal touch. It must be warm and intimate to make people feel at home. I call the other branch a home, bit of an expense to change here because parlor is in the neon sign. I feel parlor is a word that lets you down. Something poor people have. I like the word home. I don't gloom at people. I smile. Death is a reunion. And it's a pause in the life of others.'

A low corridor. Mr Vine touches Mr Christian slowly through the soft lights, soft step by soft step.

'These are the various suites. These two have their own private rest rooms. Which has been of great success. I wouldn't say it to most people but certain functions get stimulated at the passing of a cherished one. You've noticed how I've used green light and how it glows from the walls, it's a special kind of glass that makes it do that. Only kind in New York. You don't mind me showing you around.'

'No it's all right.'

'In a few years I'm opening a branch out in the country. For some people the country signifies peace. You saw that picture, the forest, In The Winter Sun. Looking at that gave me the idea. It's not conducive to peace to come in off the street. And you hear that elevated train out there. Thinking of tearing it down. Won't be too soon for me. Shake the teeth out of your head. And in here is our chapel. I thought I'd make it round just like the world and again green is my motif. And out here again there's the door to our work rooms. We call it the studio.'

'It's all very nice.'

'That makes me feel good. I'm pleased. And I hope you'll be satisfied you dealt with me. I always want people to feel that. You can trust me and know I've got reverence for my work. To love your work is happiness. It means I meet someone like you too. I'm never wrong about people. I know the real tears of death and they don't go down the cheeks. And this is my largest room, the first one I ever used. One or two personages been here. Mr Selk the manufacturer. I had that privilege. And we light a candle behind this green glass when someone is reposing. I think it gives, or rather, let me say, lends a sacredness to the occasion.'

'Yes it does.'

'You go home now. Put all bother out of your head. Get a good night's sleep. And I'm here, remember that, for any kind of request. Our car will be there in the morning. Good night, Mr Christian.'

Mr Vine and Christian shook hands. Vine gave Christian a catalogue. Pushed open the door to the cold electric light of the street. A last smile, a wave.

The windy canyon of Park Avenue. Crossing a winter city. Cold heels on the pavement. Door men rubbing hands, clicking feet, looking up, looking down the street. Beginning to snow. Like the first winter I got to Dublin. When the skies were grey for months. And I bought thick woolen blankets at the shop and they smelled like sheep.

Christian, hands plunged in pockets, takes a lonely subway west and north. Back by the shadows of the museum. And along by the stone mansions. Where I live tonight.

Music coming from the door with the name under the cellophane. Dim light in the hall, a smell of wax in the air. Dust in the nose. Door slamming. Voice yelling. Pipe down.

Must go in through this door and sleep. Pull aside the thick red curtain so tomorrow the light will wake me up. Snow streams down under the street lamp. Someone else's house is more your own if it's filled with strangers. Helen, I wouldn't have brought you to a room like this. Makes me feel I'm casting some poverty on you because this isn't the type of place you would ever be. Yours were bathrooms shining with gleaming rails and hot towels. All this plastic junk. Couldn't have been in the studio while Vine and I were talking. Couldn't talk like that. But that's the way we

45

talked. Like pies peaches or eggs. Helen's not a pie peaches or eggs. She's mine. Taking her away. Gone already. Where is she nearest to me. Asleep on top of my brain. Came with me all over the ship when I couldn't stand them staring at me everywhere I went and whispering. Our table out in the centre of the dining room. They were all thinking of the day when they had the gala occasion with the paper hats and balloons and Helen just sat there at the table and wept pink handkerchief tucked up your sleeve and pearls like tiny drops from your face and none of them ever saw you again.

They even came up to my cabin door after you were dead to listen to hear if I was crying. And the steward who said they wouldn't do your washing. He stuck his brown face in the door and closed it quietly when he saw me prostrate on the bunk. And he slammed the door in your face. Both of us utterly helpless, could do nothing could say nothing. I held the three dollars in my fist and watched his brown hand come up from his side and pull them out and leave quietly closing the door. The waiter who filled our plates with things we didn't want and came over the second day and said your wife don't eat no more and I said no. And lunchtime he came back saying he was sorry he didn't know, the wine waiter just told him and he got me a plate covered in smoked salmon. He kept as far away as he could until the last meal when hovering for his tip he asked me if I was a refugee. Went out, looked down on the strange flat shore. And in that cabin, Helen, where you left your soul and I've got to lie a night here between these sleepless sheets without you.

Sound of snow shoveling in the street. Ship's whistle from the river. Tingling and banging in the pipes along the wall. Outside the wind blows hard and shivers the window. Knocks on the door.

'Mr Christian there's a man for you down stairs.'

'Please tell him I'm coming right away.'

Christian looking into the street below. A man in dark coat, green shirt, black tie. No hat over his half bald head and grey wisps of hair. A black long car. Come for me. Can't keep him waiting. Can't stop them putting you in the ground under the snow.

Mrs Grotz at the door, hunched, breath steaming in the cold air, her hands rubbing. Watching Christian pass and meet the chauffeur halfway down the steps. A solemn soft voice and placing a black cap on his head.

'You Mr Christian. I'm from Vine funeral home.'

'Sorry to keep you waiting.'

Grotz edging her slippered feet out into the snow. Straining ears to listen. Her mouth open, eyes wide. 'Hey what's the matter. Who's hurt. Some trouble. You from a funeral.'

Christian stopping turning. Pulling gloves tighter on his hands. Looks up the steps at Mrs Grotz.

'It's my wife.'

'What's a matter, you got a wife. Where's your wife. What's a matter your wife.'

'She's dead.'

'Mister. Oh mister.'

The park ahead, little rolling hill in velvet snow. So white and Christmas. Birds taking white baths. Plows pushing it up, conveyer belts pouring it into trucks. I've no black tie. But a green one will suit Mr Vine. People we pass look at this expensive car.

'You comfortable, Mr Christian.'

'Yes thanks.'

'They're shoveling salt. Then when the snow melts the guy's tires in front shoot it up on your windshield. Some problem. They know it's going to snow every year, you'd think they'd do something.'

'Yes.'

A morning sun shining in slits along the cross town streets and in shadows across the park. These tall hotels. All so

47

slender women walk in. Where the lights glow. And everybody's scared of everybody. And maybe Vine and his personal touch.

Vine Funeral Parlor, green neon sign. Sanitation department truck stopped outside. Bedraggled men filling it with snow. Mr Vine waves his arm. Seems red in the face.

'Good morning, Mr Christian. Had to tell these men to get this garbage truck out of here. Come this way, Mr Christian.'

Vine pushing open the door, taking Christian's coat. A firm handshake, nodding his head and twitching. Shaking water out of his ears after swimming. Now he beckons the way.

'It's my favorite music I've chosen, Mr Christian. She's very beautiful. She's waiting for you. And just press the button when you want me. All right.'

'Yes.'

The room dark. Curtains drawn across the window to the street. And the green light flickering behind the glass. Casket gleaming and black. On a pedestal, the wreath illumined in green. My Helen written with the tiny white heads of lilies of the valley. A table with a Bible. Chairs along the wall for mourners. Even has my flowers lit up. He must rake in the money. I'm glad the casket's black. I'd die if it were green. Now go and kneel. So soft and I can't look at you. See just the tips of your knuckles. You don't have to shake Vine's hand, he almost broke mine. If you'd move. Encased in glass and you can't get up. Forgive me because I haven't got the courage to look at you. Because I'd see you dead forever. What happens to all the flesh and blood. No child. You leave nothing except the pain of missing you. And I didn't want the expense because a baby cost money. I wouldn't part with a penny. Only reason I had. I knew you were begging me and I'd always say let's wait. And we waited. Your casket's so smooth. Funny I put my hand along the bottom to see if it's stuck with chewing gum.

Vine would never allow that. And although he must be half crazy he's given me comfort because I don't feel you're laughed at or joked over dead. Got to keep my head down or I'll look by accident. Thought I would cry and I can't. Helen, I wish we were different from everybody else. Scream for some sort of thing that makes us you and me. Neither of us nothing. And on the ship you said you wanted to lie down in the cabin. Those first Americans you met just tired you out. And I was so proud of bringing you back to my country. I wanted you to like them. And even after you'd gone, I didn't want anyone to come and touch me on the arm and back with a pat or two and say I'm sorry about it, about your wife, have courage or something, but I did want them. I wanted someone to show something. Anything. But not a soul on that damn ship came near me except for money. And each second you get further away from me. Dig the hole with the straight sides and before it gets dark they've got you covered up. And all the times I wished you were dead. So I could be free. But they were black thoughts of anger. But I thought them. Must get up. Look out the window.

Silently crossing the room. Parting the thick curtains to the late morning light of the street. And people hunching by in the cold. Over there Murray's best for bargains. Vine said press the button when you're ready. Does he take ordinary lipstick and put it on the lips. Or take it out of a pot they use on everyone. And all sorts of lips. And make them the kind that gleam and don't have cracks. and are red and now overripe. Vine had a green handkerchief in his pocket. What has he got against the color green. Most of his life must be whispering, nodding, hand rubbing, and the five words, we'll take care of everything.

Christian turning from the window. Mr Vine leaning over the casket wiping the glass.

'Must be a little condensation on the inside Mr Christian. But I hate anything to mar such a lovely face. Woman's lips are one of the most beautiful parts of her body. I can always tell a woman who looks at a man's lips when he talks instead of his eyes. Are you all right.'

'Yes. Do you think we could leave now.'

'Yes, a few minutes. Our large reposing room is busy this morning. We never know in this business.'

'Mr Vine I think maybe you're telling me too much about your business. I don't want to say anything but it's getting me down.'

'What's the matter.'

'I don't want to know about the business. It's getting me down.'

'Don't get sore. I forget sometimes. I try to make everyone feel at home and not treat the funeral business as something strange. People ought to know about it. My own funeral is already arranged. But don't get sore. When it happened to me and it was my wife, I found I wanted some sort of distraction and because I arranged the services myself it made me feel better. And I thought you wanted to take an interest.'

'This isn't distraction.'

'Take it easy son. You're not alone in this, remember that. If I shot my mouth off, I'm sorry. I don't want to do that with nobody. But getting sore isn't going to bring her back. Beauty is the only thing you can remember. Try to remember beauty. Come on, I like you, be a sport.'

'My wife's dead.'

'I know that.'

'Well, what the hell do you mean, sport.'

'If I understand you correctly Mr Christian, you'd rather I didn't conduct this any further. I can put you in the hands of an assistant if you prefer.'

'All right, all right. I'm not the kind of person who wants to start trouble. Leave everything as it is. I'm just worried about money and what I'm going to do.'

'Look. Listen to me. I want to tell you straight. I don't

cut cash out of nobody. I don't conduct this business on those lines. You've got as long as you want and longer. Understand me. And if that isn't long enough I'll think of something. If you hadn't come here alone from another country I wouldn't take all this trouble but you seem to be a nice guy. I even thought you were a type for this profession and that's a compliment as far as I'm concerned. You're a gentleman. And when it's over, if you want to come back and see me, I'd like that. There's a place for you here, remember that. And if you make that decision, I'd like that. Shall we close it now, Mr Christian. You're ready.'

'All right.'

'You can wait with the chauffeur.'

'O.K.'

'We'll take care of you. Christian, remember this isn't death. All this is life.'

Walking out of the hall. Through the curtained doors. Putting up coat collars. The chauffeur smoking a cigarette. One of his grey wisps of hair hangs and goes into his ear. Christian coughs. Chauffeur getting out to open the door. A flash of yellow socks with white stripes.

The car pulls across the road. The hearse draws up in front of the Vine Funeral Parlor. Three men step out, rubbing their green gloved hands, stamping their feet on the hard snow. Elevated train roaring by on its iron trestle at the end of the street. The garbage truck has taken away its pile of snow. Chauffeur blows a smoke ring. And he turns around.

'Would you like this blanket, Mr Christian. Put it round your legs in case you get cold. Always a few degrees colder when you get out of the city.'

'Thanks.'

'They are coming out now, Mr Christian.'

Mr Vine standing aside, holding back a door. Coffin on four shoulders. Like an elephant, four black legs. Vine twitches his head, bends his ear to his shoulder and rubs. Goes in again. Comes out in a black overcoat, papers in

51

his hand, hatless, eyes bright. Crossing the street. Stepping gingerly with his gleaming black shoes over the ridges of snow. Leaning in the window to the chauffeur.

'To expedite the journey, John, we'll take the West Side drive. Go up Park and cross-town on Fifty Seventh. You all right, Mr Christian.'

'Yes.'

Vine pausing, a car sweeps by. He looks upon the rest of the world as something he will bury. His gravel voiced military manoeuvres. I guess we're going. No use fighting over it. He's only trying to be nice. First time anyone ever offered me a job.

Hearse pulling out. Vine signaling with his hand. And we follow. To the end of the street. Another elevated train. Wake Helen up. Window full of refrigerators there. Say they're giving them away for nothing, almost. Just step inside for bargains beyond belief. I feel like there's nothing around me in the world. Highway on the curve of the earth. Everybody knows why I'm in this car and Helen in hers.

The two black cars swiftly moved across Fifty Seventh Street. Past the opera house on the corner where people huddle up under the marquee waiting for the bus. The sky opens up where the city ends and the Hudson flows by. Up the ramp and flowing out into the stream of cars on the smooth white highway. Towering cold bridge high up over the Harlem River. Further and the red tiled roofs of houses behind the leafless trees. Along here the rich live down to the water's edge.

Road curves up through the second woods. A lake behind in the valley, a swamp and golf course. Great chains hang from post to post. Tall iron gates. Monuments inside with stained glass windows. Some with spires. Take you in here and lay you down. This cold day. Knuckles frozen. Breasts still. Where no love can taste. Tickle or tender.

Man in soft grey uniform salutes. Mr Vine steps out across

the snow. Up the steps into a grey stone building. Thin veins of ivy. Vine's coming to speak.

'There'll be a few minutes' delay. Just a formality. John, just pull the car up in front there and wait for us.'

Chauffeur turning, ice crackling under the wheels.

'It's nothing, Mr Christian. Just identification. They have to check everybody who's buried.'

Coffin on the four shoulders disappearing under the canopy and into the squat building into the side of the hill. Be looking at her again. They give us no privacy. They'd shout back at me if I object. If you own a bird and it's flown away you run out to tell the whole world. And they tell you to shut up, you're disturbing the peace.

They come out. Shift and slide it in. Engines purr and we move. All these winding roads and trees. People under the stones. So white and white. Branches frozen silver. Paths crisscrossing everywhere. Tombs on the hills. Heads in sorrow. Lightning in a sky in summer. A bronze woman melted and cold on a door. Cowled face with a hand on her cheek. Hold away the world from the rich bones inside. A white marble man and woman stand up out of their rock. Look out over a sea. Where ships die. And men slip below the cold water. And where are you nearest.

No trees here. Four men stand by the tent. They've brushed away the snow. Fake grass over the mound of earth. Norman Vine comes back to this car.

'Mr Christian. I thought since you've got no religious preference I might read something. And I've just told John to give a few dollars to the grave diggers if that's all right, it's the average tip.'

'Yes.'

'We'll go then.'

Gently sloping hill. Snow lies for miles. Fades below the stiff dark trees. High grey sky. Know young girls you love. Take cigarettes from lips and kiss. A dance band plays. Grow up loving memories. Die leaving none. Except the

Christmas Eves. When the whole year stops. These Polish hands who shovel on the dirt sit at poker tonight and drink wine. Downtown in the city. They take away a wife who clings to railings along the side walk and she screams and they lock her up. Can't see her any more because she's crazy. Love you as much as love can be. Cooking and washing. Mending and waiting. Each thread of body till it breaks.

'If you'll just stand there, Mr Christian, I'll read these few words I've got here.'

Cornelius Christian next to Norman Vine. Who holds out his little paper. Nods his head to the diggers. Straps stiffening under the coffin. Mist in the air from his voice.

'We are gathered here as brothers and we pray for another soul. The birds, trees, and flowers are life and they are around us to give birth in spring. This interment is life and for us the living, a beauty to ennoble our lives, to give us a kiss to caress us in our living pain. We gather to see the soil give one of us peace, to all love and remember her forever. We now give her to her God. O.K. boys.'

One for Yes

In a rented pair of blue tinted eyeglasses, crossing by the fish market and moving down Owl Street past the wide steps of the treasury building. The middle of the month of August. Reaching out across the weeks to sink clutching fingers into this harmless Wednesday.

On the early morning streets messengers trotting in and out of doors. Just this instant I feel good. Ships moving out to sea on the high tides. Barges carrying western trains headed north across the narrow waters. Bridges and highways humming with tires. Smell of coffee across this downtown.

I stop. Look up. Obstructing me in my forward motion, a face coming out of prepsterhood. Quickly steering a detour into the gutter, and nearly getting cut down with machines, I had to leap back from the honking horns. Too late, too weak and vulnerable to turn and run this crazy time in my personal history. A smooth jawed figure. Grey natty topcoat, cream shirt and fat striped tie. And eyes that turned on their glow.

'I know you, hey aren't you George Smith. Not so fast like you were at the building site, that time.'

'Beep.'

'Ha you're George Smith all right.'

'Beep.'

'What do you mean, beep for an old friend. We were prepsters together.'

'Beep.'

'Ha ha George. It is you. Greetings. No kidding. Well

how are you. I read that nifty write up in the papers. I mean
you're a somebody. I mean I'm not doing badly. I'm doing
all right. Got myself a little old partnership. But I mean how
are you, all right.'

'Beep beep.'

'Now wait a minute. George ha ha. I know this is a funny
situation.'

'Beep.'

'But a jokes a joke. O.K.'

'Beep beep.'

'Now hold it. Let's not make a meeting like this in the
middle of Owl Street with all the congestion, holding things
up. I mean you're located here. What do you say.'

'Beep.'

'Gee George is there something wrong. Are they crowding you. This has kind of gone on too long to be comic. I
can take a hint, if that's it. What are you saying this beep to
me for. If you don't want to recognise me say so.'

'Beep beep.'

'What is it. Is this a method, something happened and you
use this method. I mean they said in the papers you were
building a mausoleum, that costs, I know, I mean are you
nervous.'

'Beep.'

'It's a method.'

'Beep.'

'I see that's one beep. O now I remember. The rude noise
you made to the reporters. O I'm catching on, a voice lapse.
It's one beep, maybe, for yes.'

'Beep.'

'And two for no.'

'Beep.'

'I'm sorry, I didn't know anything about this George. Is
it permanent.'

'Beep.'

'Gee that's tough, on your wife and kids. I heard you got

married. Only guessing you got kids. To Shirl. What a girl. She'd never even gave me a tumble. Remember the tea dances. Those white linen suits Shirl used to wear. She was beautiful.'

'Beep.'

'But I just didn't know you had this problem. I guess you're under specialists.'

'Beep.'

'New method like this must tax the mind. You must want to really say something once in awhile. Like an opinion.'

'Beep beep.'

'Is that right. If there's anything you need. I know you have money. But if you're bothered by a problem, spiritual, you know. Why you holding your hand to your ear. You're not deaf too.'

'Beep.'

'O, gee, that's tough. You lip read.'

'Beep.'

'You remember Alice. You know I married her.'

'Beep beep.'

'She only mentioned you the other day. How Shirl followed you right across the ocean. The ocean. I'm saying the ocean. My Alice, yes, mentioned you. She mentioned you. This is a really rotten world. Real rotten. It's rotten. Guy's speech and hearing cut off in his prime. I said in your prime. It's a shame. But you can still see. I said see, you can still see. To lip read. From behind the blue glasses.'

'Beep.'

'Thank God for that. Can they do something for you. I said, help you. Can they help you.'

'Beep beep.'

'It makes you sick, doesn't it. A disgrace. I said it was a disgrace.'

'Beep.'

'Believe me I'm really sorry for what's happened to you. I mean that sincerely. I said, I'm sorry. Sincerely.'

'Beep beep beep.'

'That's three. I got it. For thanks.'

'Beep.'

'Only George, I'm sort of in a hurry. Like to hang on, talk over old times. Sure would like to hear. I mean, get together won't we. I mean sometime, old sport, when you're all right again. You'll be all right. Thing is not to worry. I said, don't worry. Looking at my watch. Got to be dead on time, somewhere. An appointment. I wish you all of God's luck that someday you may be well again. Hope your health comes back. I mean that.'

'Beep beep beep.'

'Sorry I got to rush. But if you can read my lips I'm saying the cure may be in prayer George. Pray. So long.'

'Beep beep beep beep.'

'Ha ha, goodbye.'

'Beep.'

'See you.'

'Beep beep beep beep.'

A Friend

Before a Christmas in the hard frosty month. They said on the telephone he was dead. I went over to church and sat downstairs in the back in the singing and incense. I thought of summer and the maple leaves. And how they grow there to make tunnels of the streets. And if you die you go away up somewhere in the sky where the airplanes are and it's white and blue. And it's red and gold.

They had to bring him back from Florida and all the sunny months. Where the big bugs bang the windows and the golf courses have spongy grass. Loading him in the train on the lonely night north, wrapped in a flag. Over his cold blond smile.

I go back on the slate sidewalk set in the stone ground and kids' marble holes worn shallow. As children here we were Catholics come together. And altar boys trying to touch God. Stealing apples and cherries Saturday. Sunday adoring the Holy Ghost. Sat out nights on rivers, skating on lakes in the moon. And each summer getting black in the sun and chasing through the waves. He'll be on the train crossing Virginia through Emporia on that flat sea level land. Over Maryland and the dark green hills. And then Newark where beyond the swamps are the thin white sparkling things sticking in the night and how you go in that endless tunnel and the river crushing my ears and come out rumbling by the long platforms to a stop. They'll slide him down and wheel him to a truck with a soldier standing by. The lights will be sad and the flag will be bright. Someone will be there to meet him. And they'll take him north again to the Bronx.

And so I walk up here and near the woods where we trapped, shot squirrel and caught snakes by the tail. Tied a big swing sky high in the oak that I never dared try. Everything green in a fat sun. Each girl friend was forever in talks through the night on some fence. When we washed ears and polished face, hair and shoes until they were health. And we went places where we said hi there, isn't it swell we all met like this. A game played with hearts and fingertips. Then he had moved away during the war to where there were no trees and lives of people on top of lives and more beside more, in hallways holding grey tiles, footsteps of strangers and silence.

On the hard sad day. I drove down the avenue under the roaring elevator train. And parked in a side quiet street of gloom and grey. I ask the man at the door and he said softly the Lieutenant is reposing in suite seven to your right along the corridor. His name up on a little black sign with moveable white letters that slide on for the next and next. I shake hands and nod with these other friends. Some smile beneath their crinkled eyes and say it's good to have you here. I kneel at the casket to pray. Always the holiest hearts are dead. Yet he had punched me in the mouth when I had braces on my teeth and crushed my model airplane. And I had loved his sister. In there under glass where I don't want to look.

Next morning mass and casket and people stepping out into the dreary cold. And a long line of black cars went north again to the cemetery they called the Gate of Heaven. I was the last car filled with his girl friends and sniffles. Off the highway and up a mountain road past the hot dog stand, a few last gold leaves wagging on the trees, and white islands of snow spaced through the woods.

The little green tent and fake rolls of grass they spread over the dirt. The diggers go behind the grave stones to put on caps and jackets, a great heavy row of European hands hanging from the smooth covert cloth. The soldiers lined up and let go a sudden crack in the sky and the bugle with its death sounds going down the valley and coming back again from the hills around.

I stood behind some people and never saw him going down. His girl friends cried and one screamed and was held away and she knelt, her nylon knees sinking in the mud, and we all began to pray and say things to ourselves.

Dear Sylvia

I am writing this letter, you know why. It wasn't that your mother ripped the curtains down but that she was attacking me with a lethal weapon which, if nothing else, shows she's got no respect for me and I am, after all, your husband. I would have hit my own mother under similar circumstances, God rest her soul.

I think you overlook the fact that I am a college graduate who majored in chemistry and it's not that I'm trying to blow my own horn but you ought to remember that I've got more brains than your whole family of farmers. You sent for them, not me. If it were to have been a little family chat that's all right, but to be beaten up in my own house that's another thing. Something worse could have happened than a mere broken hip. What was I expected to do against three, especially when they had your key and planned to get me in bed, defenseless. Putting vaseline over the floor was not the act of a coward but a strategist. Admittedly I never dreamed it would work so well.

Right, so they're going to sue me for damages but I want to know how your father is going to explain coming into the apartment with a hay rake, fifty miles from the nearest field. Rake up the grass in our window boxes? So you see I'm not in the least worried. And remember this, when your brother slipped and broke his hip, the red bowl you bought last year in the village had just left his hand, which he claimed, rather prematurely I thought, was the arm that pitched eight no hit games for Erasmus High and of course he promptly pitched on his backside courtesy my vaseline.

It was only his screams of agony which prevented your brother Tim and father from beating me up although with greasy feet they too might have ended up in the hospital.

And don't forget to tell your father's lawyer that I, as the occupier of 4-F, don't have to warn parties who are trying to murder me in my bed that they are open to risks inside my door. Which makes me call to mind the nasty references that were made to the number of my apartment during the war. To imply that I was classified as 4-F and unfit for service is a slander on my physical health which has always been, if I do say so myself, superb. I was prevented from active duty by the nature of my work at college and I don't care if you never believe me. There were some people who did more to win the war back in the States than a thousand like your brothers who as far as I can gather were charging every bush and stump in Hawaii with fixed bayonets which in the end were used only to open beer cans.

But this is not a letter of recrimination. Far from it. I just want you to get the facts straight and understand my side of it. I've never held anything against your family except that remark about my parents being ignorant immigrants. They were hard working, clean living, good people who saw to it that I got the opportunities they never had and slaved and sacrificed so I could be what I am today. Even so, sometimes my dear Sylvia, I can't help feeling a little relieved that I've only been one generation in this great land.

But as I've said, this is not a letter of recrimination. Although your constant accusations that I was cheap, tight-wad and the rest never helped matters. This business of the sun shade for the car is a fad and just because I don't want to get one doesn't mean that I'm a tightwad. You ought to realise that people who really have something don't go around advertizing it to everybody. Sure, laugh at those old guys riding bicycles around Boston but every time you make a telephone call that rings up a little something on their dividends.

And this is something I really mean. I'd like to be friends with your brothers and it's not because I'm scared of them. I studied jujitsu in a course at college and was recommended for further training. But for my part I'd like to forget everything. However, none of this would have happened if your mother had minded her own business in the beginning. Offering me a job feeding pigs is no way to talk to someone who was in the top half of his class right through college. And then to come into our apartment and call me a red because of the color of the curtains is going too far.

I've had my say and have set out the facts in a broad-minded way and as far as I'm concerned the whole incident is a thing of the past. If you want I'll meet you at Grand Central, seven, Sunday and we could have meat balls and spaghetti at Joe's. Alone.

Your loving husband,
Hugo

Dear Hugo

I hope this letter finds you as sick as your letter made me. You're so smart aren't you? No one can tell you, can they? I wish you could find something new to brag about because I'm getting tired hearing you were in the first half of your class right through college. I guess that's where you learned to hit women and to beat a fast retreat when someone your own size comes along. And don't give me that foolishness that my mother tried to attack you with a lethal weapon. Ever since we've been married you've tried to make trouble over her. She's my mother and has a perfect right to come and see me when she wants and to comment on the curtains.

But don't you go around trying to paint yourself as my brave husband because I heard a different story. When my father and brothers came in the door to get you, as you put it, they said you went to get under the bed and even after Joe slipped and broke his hip. Putting vaseline on the floor wasn't the work of a coward but a strategist? What a laugh, it's killing me. That's how brave you are. Why couldn't you take your beating like a man instead of trying some dirty trick like that. Just the type of thing I'd expect too. And boy how you exaggerate. My father's hay rake was in the back of the truck all the time and don't worry he wouldn't need the help of a hay rake to take you on, you can be sure of that. And just one item you overlooked, it was you who threw the red bowl because the janitor was just putting out the garbage and he heard you screaming, 'And you can take your sister's red bowl too, right in the head.' So think that over before you dream up any more for your action of assault.

And you don't know how wonderful it is to get a letter from you in which you're so eager to get the facts straight and to set them out in a broadminded way. I'm sure your head must be at least two feet between the ears, remind me to measure it sometime.

And no one ever said anything about your parents being ignorant immigrants, I just said they were immigrants and hadn't caught on yet which is only natural seeing as they came from a pretty backward country which, of course, I'm not saying is their fault. But just like you to give me that stuff you're relieved to be only one generation here and if that's so I don't see you breaking a leg to get the boat back. But maybe that's your mission in life to go back there with your chemistry degree and show them how to smarten up. I notice you always have a lot of bright ideas how we can modernize the apartment and that great invention of yours for drying hair which almost electrocuted me which maybe was what you were trying to do. Anyway we all know what a big time genius you are, especially the smooth way you wash dishes.

But I love that, your family slaved and sacrificed so that you could be what you are today – pardon me while I mail them a medal. What do you call fooling round with a lot of smelly little explosions for eighty dollars a week that my father and brothers make selling a few hogs. And you were insulted because they offered you a job feeding them and only because they wanted to give you a break and didn't want to see me cooped up in that sweat box. And I might add it would have been the highest paid job you've ever had.

Honestly you make me tired. And that is something that better be understood before I come back. You've spent the last five dollars you're going to, having your accent lifted by that red bearded maniac. The way he comes bouncing in with that stupid tape recorder reciting his high brow poems

66

sounding like a Boston over-baked bean. Who do you think it impresses? He's the one who's put all these crazy ideas in your head and all that accent will get you is a sock on the jaw and maybe a few days in jail. All of which might do you some good. But you're not pulling these old fashioned ideas on me, the housework is fifty fifty and that's final.

So I've had my say too and am willing to forget the incident as well. But if I meet you at Grand Central on Sunday, I'm certainly not going to Joe's for spaghetti and meat balls, you don't buy me off with a cheap manoeuvre like that. Otherwise I take the train straight back – alone.

Your loving wife,
Sylvia

Party on Saturday Afternoon

He had a tin can on the end of a string, swinging it around his dark skull, bored. The other kids were throwing a ball against a high wall, scattering after it, a melody of dirty words. Israel's dark brown backside was sticking out of his short pants. He was the thinnest in the gang. Then there was Rinso. Rinso could run like a deer. He had big dark eyes that opened like an owl's when someone described strawberry shortcake to him. A.K., one eyed A.K., the only white boy in the gang, was the one who was always telling Rinso luscious stories about strawberry shortcake. A.K. loved to watch the thin dark boy's eyes grow big, his big mouth open like elevator doors, while telling him about the great cake his mother was going to have ready that night, Saturday night. A.K. knew he was telling a big lie, and that the cakes he described were only pictures in a magazine. But he liked his friend Rinso so much that he wouldn't disappoint him when he begged A.K. to tell him about the dessert his mother was going to have that night.

'Cum mon dere, A.K., you-all tell dis boy what youh mammy done gonna fill your belly wit ta'night.'

'No,' A.K. answered with downcast eyes, kicking a tin can, feeling all the misery of being dishonest with his best friend.

'Cum on, A.K., what yuh all stallin' fouh? I is just gettin' mah mouth ready for this dream meal.'

'No. No more, I'm not gonna tell you any more – for reasons – for personal reasons.'

'Well, den, A.K., I guess maybe yuh all don't wanna

come to dis here party Measles' given in his house dis very afternoon.'

A.K. looked up suddenly, suspiciously.

'What party? I ain't heard of any party of Measles'. You can't kid me. There's no party.'

'Well, iffen youh don't believe me, youh don't have to. You're not even supposed to know about dis here party.'

A.K. was eager now. His eyes fastened upon Rinso in a stare. Rinso did not waver, and A.K. knew he was telling the truth.

'But listen, A.K., don't tell anyone I done told you.'

A.K. interrupted – 'But why didn't Measles ask me if he asked everyone else?'

'Don't ask me,' Rinso shrugged, 'all I know it dat youh done got to bring a present. Maybe Measles forgot ta ask you – you know how dumb Measles is sometimes.'

A.K. looked around the lot. 'Where's Measles?' he yelled.

'He's gone home,' someone shouted.

A.K. hastened away down the street, with visions of Meales' party that afternoon. He could see the table laden with chocolate cake, pop corn and jelly beans. What would he bring for a present. He remembered the four store bottles on the back porch. That was 12 cents. He would go to Woolworth's five and dime after lunch and find something special.

In Woolworth's he looked all over the toy and gun counter. He could find nothing. Then on the stationery counter he spied a ten-cent globe of the world. Just the thing. He began to see Measles' eyes getting big – his would be the best present there. He thought of the table, chocolate cake, jelly beans and pop corn.

He looked at the clock. Ten minutes after two. The party would be started by now, he'd better hurry. He ran a hundred yards, walked a hundred yards, as he had been taught in the Boy Scouts.

As he rang the bell he could see dark figures moving

behind the curtains. He felt his heart beating more quickly. He wondered what he'd say if Measles' mother opened the door. They were taking a long time. He held the globe behind his back. Through the curtains, he could make out Rinso's face looking out. The door began to open. It was Israel.

'A.K., you can't come in here.'

'Why not.'

'A.K. you're white, you know dat.'

A.K. retreated down the steps. Inside, he could see Rinso's face turn away.

Whither Wigwams

I have had some sad times in this country. But I have grown accustomed to the routine. I would like the public houses to be open all the time and for the smoke to be abated. Last night I was dreaming of escape. With several nationalities after me, and various types. I can't quite remember if any of these were British. On the other hand, the British are always after you. In their quiet persistent way. Old women to see if you beat your children. The entire middle class to catch you cheating on the train. The aristocracy, God bless and keep them always, mind their own business. Otherwise, living in England is very cosy indeed.

I am located in Fulham, down an upper working class street, living as honourably as anyone can in this naughty world. I've shouted loudly once or twice at the neighbours, remonstrating with them for giving some rather sneaky abuse to my children. I am glad to say my kids now play freely in front of the house. My hard eye is suspicious of the disreputable and reputable alike. This is the behaviour of a New Yorker, which I am. But I am shy and thrive on people being nice to me and with friends I am found to be open, honest, warm, to the point of sheer insanity at times.

Now for the embarrassing statement, resented by the human and inhuman alike. I write for a living. I used to think in my early and generous days that anyone could do this. But they can't. And how I have managed for these last ten or so years I will never know, but about six of them I have spent variously in Britain. Where they have mostly heard of me under counters and behind doors until recently. And of course, some are shocked to see me, full of friendliness and nearly wracked with humility, reluctantly accepted as a writer. Regrettably there seems to be no category for me, and the situation is rather awkward. Type after type presents himself splay footed, looking me up and down for any frayed cuff, to ask how much money I make and is it enough to live on. It is this materialism which makes me so sad. There is no romance, no glory that you as a writer sat down and bravely sweated on the white sheets. Of paper. To create something.

This is where Ireland comes in handy. I feel that there they look into your eyes. It may take three hours and ten pints but finally they look into your eyes, put a hand over the bar, shake the head and say, a grand book. And then it's my chance to say, I'm glad I wrote it. And then they say just as quickly, Ah well, then I'm glad I read it. Now this is pleasant. And money is never mentioned. So long as you buy the next round. O beautiful Irish days in Dublin. Which I was sorry to recently hear is sinking at the rate of a foot a year into the sea. Sad news for me, especially with the people so devout.

In this London city I frequently go to Harrods. Where I tread the nice carpets and stand perusing in the various departments, especially that of the meat, fish and poultry. Here I ridiculously lurk for hours. And it is a tribute to those chaps behind the counter who may whisper about me but tolerate my long presence absolutely. A harmless occupation looking at the crabs, lobster, salmon, game and beef. It's almost as if the fields, rivers and shores where these creatures were killed were there and one sniffs a wild rural breeze.

I confess to looking over the customers as well. From here I almost invariably go to the glass department, being a modest collector of the hand blown quality and order a few. Then to the music department for an eyeful of soothing harpsichords. Hovering over the brown veneer, perhaps a finger tenderly touching an ivory key. And a world opens up, the summer evening, the lily smell, the garden and tinkle of the village church bell as I sit playing obscurely.

How I love romance and vines and vintage. But wait. My ear catches an altercation. I hear several clipped indignant words. What a pity to come back into the clash of egos being shaped, bolstered, misshapen, crushed, kicked, stepped on, trammelled. I take mine, which is so vulnerable, away to the marble waiting hall and there sit in one of the green leather chairs, legs crossed, socks pulled up, waiting. I sometimes think that someone will smile and come and meet me. But no. Curiosities stroll by, starlets carrying dogs, dowagers with canes and sometimes a naughty looking solicitor. And the afternoon is closing. The sales staff get that inspired vigour which comes with locking up and go sprightly to and fro. I am always mesmerised by this display of enthusiasm at this time of day. Jauntily I go on the streets again, walking in random directions. Watch the lonely respectable people come back to their dark bed sitters and stare into the basements, up at roofs and through any open door.

In the mostly grey of London I wake up in the morning in the front bedroom, usually at six because two women go by on their way to work at the laundry at the end of the road. If I'm lucky I go back to sleep again and my breakfast comes to me with the mail at nine. Most mail leaves me staring at my walls and out the window and at the chimneys of the bakery across the street. My thoughts are sometimes of the past, of Ireland and Dublin, of the windswept drunken nights on the various country roads. Of the jaws one tried to hit as they flashed by and a defenceless woman caught it instead, collapsing in a moaning heap twenty yards away. With the knowing whispers of the crowd, ah it was an accident but didn't she deserve it and have it coming, ah the hand of God comes out of the night itself and plays havoc with those who need teaching a good lesson. The mad parties, the like of which had never been seen before and not since. Of two types. One where the evening was jolly and ended up with the wielding of bottles. The other where it was sad and ended up with the wielding of bottles.

Then I think of my own culture and America. Of the open wild greenery. The trees. Of the sad lives of my childhood friends as they grew up in that land of opportunity. And found you grow as your parents. That dad was not God or even a good salesman, but a trembling, terrified man in a nightmare. The neighbours fighting their own little wars out of sight in the kitchen over the crumb cake and container of milk. As the sons said, I'm going to make a million, mom. Goodness, the beer quaffed on these occasions. For myself I never guaranteed making more than fifty thousand. But over the kitchen table and dining room I grew up. But lived in a musical world alone in my bedroom. The boyhood plots laid in sweltering summer attics, digging through cheap heirlooms. Never hunger, rarely sorrow or any death. Just lawns, lakes and tennis. I liked it. I loved it. An exquisite dream. Spruce trees growing their blue tips to touch windows and little hills and mountains for miles around and lakes clear and magic. But maybe I knew I would leave this little community and perhaps not inherit the cars, highways, tinkling ice and tastes of beer. And on a whim one summer day I left to go to a university in Europe. Into a moral shock. Where sin was a test of natural aristocracy. Naturally I passed.

And when I went back seven years later. Big ship moving up the Hudson into the banners and bunting, greetings and sadness. My my. The straw haired, brown skinned girls of childhood, wracked on their marriage beds, weeping into a future of a husband's fat belly. And to give them their due, they had courage, and jumped off the bridge in front of the train. Others merely said cohabitation was for animals. Then I think it's sad sometimes that I didn't stay and be tragic with them. Or at least to down a few beers in the local saloon with the retarded and failed. But they were terrified at my open talk about life, and in the end I just walked by on the street outside to catch a glimpse of these boyhood friends who had been full of dreams somewhat like my own and I knew, as they bent against the bar, that they were doing the proper thing taking to drink. The trouble was that they could not admit as I could that it was not funny, although, if they could, it could be hilarious.

But I do remember one night. A few days before one of my departures by ship from New York. I was with two almost dear friends early on this cold crisp December afternoon. There was a pantry full of Irish whisky. And the air was brimming with Christmas and bright wrappings of presents. One nearly dear friend was a man, the other a woman. Alas, all three of us had escaped from Europe to the new world. We had gone back to our bubbling long cars. Smooth New York State wines. Nights that were all night. And the cultivated utter richness that is New York. I walked tweedily into the pantry. The man friend was talking to the woman friend. They were saying over the tall icy glasses, my God, let's both find a port in this storm. Cuba. Or the Bahamas.

My man friend wearing sandals and white socks, having broken his shoes kicking some door down in a rage. I had a bandaged arm, torn open having plunged my fist through a window. And this pretty woman looked a thin picture of death. Between the white cupboards of the pantry we stood smiling at each other. They looked at me and said at least you're saved in a few days by the good ship Franconia. I said it was true. On that good ship I was going down the North River and out on the cool waters. Next stop Ireland. There was a great friendly clutching of arms and bodies. We were all nearly wailing. She screamed let's all find a port quick. And my man friend of course, was taking on fuel. Called Power's Gold Label. In the long drawing-room a madrigal played. Suddenly they were on the telephone, long messages, obscure, confused, to friends back in Europe. And less confused messages to the steamship lines. They were going to escape. We went back into the long room with some sun through the window and lay back on the soft couches.

On the distant streets the sirens wailed on their way to the various slayings. I said to my man friend, it's a runaway horse, no one in control. He agreed. And I knew of his own pathetic steps to adapt. The tent he had built over his bed. The gallon bottles of Chianti he had taken with him inside while wearing his long underwear. And how he had borrowed my photographs of our days in Ireland and took them into this wigwam perusing them with tears streaming down his face.

Down ten floors on the street the cars floated by, all day, all night, all noon and afternoon. One made contact by telephone across the city, Bronx, Brooklyn and Canarsie. I could hear him in his wigwam, out of which he refused to come for days at a time and could only be reached by talking machine. I said my God, come out of there, I told him that this behaviour which I could understand so well and in fact encouraged at first, would only put the wind gale force up his ivy league friends with whom he shared the apartment. And sure enough they got the medicos in the white coats to come and slip on the straight jacket. But I explained to these medical people that he was not off his rock but on his rock while in his wigwam. They tried to lock me up too, until I said I had diplomatic immunity, which while they checked on it, I neatly slipped into the subway.

And so now, on the December day, after these prolonged misunderstandings with various authorities, we had dinner. Guests arrived. Although rather painful, there was some laughter and gaiety. When suddenly a man who had written a play which flopped in Chicago left a table where I was, in anger, because he said I had no right to leave America and live in Europe. That in this city and country the evolution of the race had come, that I belonged to it and came out of it. He stood shaking his fist as the group feasted, and I with European aplomb was scooping up the caviar, as he shouted, if you are as good a writer as you probably are, you have no right to leave America. I was amazed as he stormed out, leaving behind his tasty victuals. Then I sat silent and impressed. He was quite right. I had no right to leave America. And I looked at my man friend and woman friend who knew I was saving my life. Which I didn't get a chance to tell him.

So I think it is a strange thing to be American. To have a sprawling mind. To have no tiger teeth for ripping enemies. Mine are intact. To have sympathy and understanding instead. And survive by bland, sheepish manoeuvring. I usually love their company and voices. And the tales of fellowships upon which they embark, sailing merrily for Europe. They are more human, urbane than the crafty types on this Atlantic side. And given to sentiment one can only have when you know what it is to own the carpet and refrigerator. But for me, the crystal loneliness of America is its greatest beauty. The wide Middle West. An area from which I've received transatlantic telephone calls at 4 a.m. which I can't answer because they're reversing the charges. And I learn it's someone in Dayton, Ohio, called Chad. And I know in my heart that Chad is a nice person whoever it is, but alas my flintiness which lurks in me from my Galway mother will not let me pay pounds for the call.

But it is gratifying that there are these men and women in America who will cry out to Europe in some telephone box, perhaps at midnight on a straight road, through the cornfields. My, what romancing. I would have advised him immediately to erect the wigwam. But I get carried away by the twang and cornfed introspection of these people. How they go East to New York, marry a girl from Radcliffe College who, during her first married year goes tight in the mind and finally screaming and clawing her way stark mad into an institution. Hanging on the railings as they drag her to Bellevue. And this tragedy is so true it has beauty. And the husband stands and tells you this and says it doesn't matter, I didn't love her. And his words are true and sad and beautiful.

But where in New York can I have the quiet ablution after breakfast, when I listen to the sometimes naughty rhythms of Housewives' Choice and go contented to my desk to add more words to my fabulous little collection. Or perhaps eleven on a spring morning to bus to the Victoria and Albert Museum and walk the almost country peace of the corridors. Take a sniff of balmy air in the central garden court of cherry blossoms. All the meanness leaves me momentarily. I think that I will never go back to live in America, in a dry wooden house wearing clean socks. But I miss the change of seasons and how death can come from anywhere. And perhaps, too, the days when I sat at a desk writing there. And at one o'clock on cool clear afternoons to go out to the corner drug store and buy a New York Times. Always noticing the girl behind the counter, who has a curious freckled roasted skin. I take a bus past the cemetery, which after the fights and fury of some of my New York nights, was the only place I would meet this friend of mine who lived in the wigwam over his bed. I'd mention the grave of some illustrious person of which there were many, and in this empty peaceful paradise of the dead, I'd see him sitting scratching his head on this gravestone as I approached stealthily from behind others. Before we could get anywhere with the conversation he'd ask me to lend him a dollar.

'My dear Mike, could you slip me one dollar of American currency.'

'No.'

'Please don't say that word.'

'I'm saying it.'

'I must have a dollar to have freedom of transport or else they will catch me.'

'We're safe here with the dead.'

'You think so.'

'Yes.'

'I'll tell you. As I strolled between these trees and lovely mausoleums I came to an open area. For some reason I said to myself, don't cross this open area someone will see you. I distinctly had the feeling I was going Asiatic. And so I stepped out into this glade. I got half way across and from the other side stepped a man. To this man I owed half a crown, which I'd borrowed three years ago in the shade of Epping Forest. Needless to say we passed each other without speaking. And fortunately he began running.'

There was commiserating about how much more of this life in our native land we could stand. I too now had a wigwam over my bed. And a few days ago, when this friend was foolish enough to venture from his wigwam, he walked clean off a subway platform at 4 a.m. while reading Berkeley's Immaterialism. And the trouble wasn't so much that he was lying unconscious between the tracks but that when they dragged him up and took a look at the book he clutched they said he was a case for Bellevue Psychiatric. Only his impetuous British accent saved him and he was dismissed as an Englishman who read books.

So I suppose I am too old to live in a wigwam but this is the secret to survival in the U.S.A. And those times when I stood on some promontory looking at New York, dumbfounded at its beauty. But then narrowing down lives till you get where they really are, over the cornflakes and facing the woman who has become a man because men are weak. But what does it matter when you are in the Bronx Zoo as I nearly always was in those days and you walk seeing the monkeys and a man comes up to you and says barefaced right into your own sad face, say buddy, what a roué you'd be back at the asylum. This I think was the friendliest thing I had said to me in that land. And when I had thought over the remark I rushed to find him for the address but he was now out in the middle of the road stopping all traffic, explaining he was an officer of the law and the road was closed to all except those on scooters.

The days ticked by. Sirens wailing. And it was a great feeling to know that the good ship Franconia was down there purring at its dock, loading on the victuals. My friend phoned me from his wigwam and said he would settle for travelling in one of my trunks. I said I couldn't arrange such a desperate thing. Then it became three days to go. There was no more word from the wigwam. I had lost my voice. And now only wrote messages on scraps of paper. I literally sat at my desk holding on. I kept my shades down so no one could draw a bead on me from across the road. I counted the minutes and hours away. At three o'clock in the afternoon it was time to go. Thinking of the lonely Irish roads. Of tea, cabbage, bacon and egg. I was chauffeured down the West Side Drive. I could see the stacks of the good ship Franconia with wisps of smoke. The sky red and raw. Everything became so simple. Just climb some wooden steps. Along the pier, put a passport into a little kiosk. I admit that I expected a hand to grab me by the wrist and say, wait a minute bud you ain't going nowhere. But the man smiled. I wrote thank you on one of my scraps of paper. I went up the gangway. They were serving tea in an enclosure called the garden lounge. There were tears in my eyes. I said silently, I'm in England. Then I watched the mooring lines. I had to see them cast off and then I would take a nice lungful of air, now that I had indeed escaped. Safe and sound on that fantail. I thought of that sad wigwam from which one of the most ferocious battles on the American continent had been waged, high over the speeding endless cars crossing the wasteland of Queens. I wondered then, whither goest that wigwam. Mine was neatly packed in the hold of the ship.

Now the blast of the ship's whistle. Echoing back from across the New Jersey shore and off the high buildings. I crouched into my fur collar. I had Cabin 38 on R deck on this nearly empty ship. That good skipper was up on his bridge. Being a naval man myself I could see all was secure for sea. Then there was that silence, that pause that precedes all momentous things, all final things. Whither goest that wigwam. The sailors' hands on the gangway waiting to let go. I heard footfalls. Rapid ones pounding closer on the wooden pier. I heard a voice I knew, shouting, don't go, wait for me. There he was, wily wigwam strapped on his back. Arran islander's hat on head. A paper bag full of a handful of possessions. An arm clutching the gallon of Chianti.

On the stern of that ship that day we stood watching. Moving out toward the Narrows. A mist over Manhattan. A deck porter handed out the beef tea and biscuit. Something had stopped in that city. It was as certain as anything I had ever felt in my life. And I knew what it was. They had stopped chasing us. Whither goest that wigwam.

Rackets and Riches at Wimbledon

In June in a thick green summer valley. The sun pours down and they pop the fluffy white ball back and forth. The little grass arenas where they say deuce and love and first service and fault and quiet please. And I go bathe myself in the intolerable sadness all sport brings to my soul.

These tasty days of The Lawn Tennis Championships upon the lawns of The All England Club. Wimbledon fortnight of golden female legs. On court and off. And I came on my own white ones which I used lightly walking down a country lane past houses with lanterns polished and gleaming outside their freshly painted doors. Where grey haired ladies take tea on their terraces and children's voices come through the air of the quiet afternoon. And by the roadside a man sits benignly playing I Know That My Redeemer Liveth on his portable organ, an upturned hat on the grass for clinking silver.

The stadium looms dark green and ivy clad, holding rich hearts, eager hearts and my own grey one shortly arriving. Into the long concrete covered tunnel to pay five shillings. Through the turnstile where the money is piling up in mountains and suddenly one stands terribly interested in a corridor thick with the tinted tender tempting smell of women. The perfume is musk and mad. Prices of the various smells pass me by at about thirty guineas an ounce. The flowered dresses, the bronze and freckled faces. Pearls and gracious beads. Hats straw and gay and striped and strange. A blond star of stage, a famous fair lady floating by, as heads turn and my mind mentions, please, may I touch you.

But she's gone with smiles only for close friends, mostly ticket holders in the shade with cushions for bottoms and backs. And her beauty goes to sit a flower among the tan masks. I squeeze bereft into the free standing room. A sardine in the sun.

Two o'clock. I'm crushed by school girls reading programmes over each other's shoulders. All in uniforms. They shove and push me with absolutely no regard for my age. I'm confused by their early interest in tennis. Perhaps parents steering them away from men. The judges come out. Wearing red and some, yellow carnations, exuding rectitude in all directions. A grassy law court. Litigants wear white. The referee takes his measuring rod to the net. Photographers preparing cameras. Ball boys in their purple and green shirts, splay footed, hands folded behind backs. They've been trained to notice a player's whim, his nod, wink and wish. And I fear, to absorb growls at the odd time when his ill nature rears.

And then suddenly there's clapping. From under the Royal awninged box come the players. Traversing silently, snugly on their soft soles. Some lilt, some bounce. There is very little waddling due to the speed of this sport. But players come in all types and sizes, or all sorts of caprice and demeanours. There are the grass beaters, who fluff the return of a lob and hold the grass down with one hand and batter it with a racket with the other. Then the kneelers. They get down on knees, putting racket gently aside to slowly hold their heads in their hands. I rather prefer this sort. They don't damage the court and it's moving to watch supplication proffered to the open sky.

But let us play tennis. There is no eagerness to start the game. At this stage they cavort with some real snazzy shots, wearing indifference on the face. Until the umpire aloft on his high chair, score sheet on his lap, whispers into the mike, are you ready. The ball boys lift the lid of the refrigerator. The balls come out, cool to the touch, bouncing with

83

perfection. Just ripe for players who come from all corners of the globe to play with these fuzzy spheres at a universal temperature. The idea is hypnotizing. And for two weeks I waited for someone to object to a warm ball.

The call for silence please. Lights lit in the scoreboard. All eyes on this sacred carpet of green. Ball boys on one knee at the net, ready to rush and scoop up on the run. Server casually to base line to carefully place a foot, and takes that instant of aim. I feel a message go to his opponent, I say chap, if you see this one at all, don't be foolish enough to stick your cat gut out because it will go right through. The player receiving the message crouches, a little flex of calf muscles and a bounce. Stares back, an eye on each side of his bat and sends back, my dear fellow I hope when my return lob passes from a ray of sunshine through your own cat gut you will be good enough to help them dig it out of your court. Needless to say not many in the crowd catch these wordless exchanges, which frankly are shockingly unspeakable between women competitors.

But there is sportsmanship. The backslap is there. For the loser at the net. The steel handshake of a winner. The arm around the shoulder walking off court. And in the heat of the match the acknowledging hand at the beauty of a drop shot. At this latter the crowd roars and claps, the executor of such a shot drops head and with humility humming, wipes face of all expression. This tells the crowd you've seen nothing yet. Which makes me long for those full women who brazenly and breastfully hammer the ball in all directions and helplessly lose.

Day after day the eliminations go on. The angled cross court passing shot much favoured by the crowds. More and more the folks gravitate to centre and number one courts. Outside in the grounds now deserted by famous names, the people thin out. The first opening week seems far away when the crowds returned fresh, gay, packed on the underground train with their cocktail chatter of voices, the lean unmuscled arms of carefree women hanging everywhere. When I heard conversation about the wine champagne and trunks for travelling and the good old days when people knew their place. And when I listened for a word of tennis and heard that an aunt Mirabelle had to let her second gardener go. I was alas, also amazed by the absolute indifference shown to my presence on the train.

And the evenings of these last days is a terrible time of sadness. Sun setting beyond the stands and further in the tips of trees. I suppose it's because Wimbledon will go on without me. I stand leaning against a fence watching the players leave. Hair neat, faces shower fresh as they wait for their chauffeured cars. All this youth beauty and bounce. On the verge of a tear I heard a cry go up from behind me near the water tower on an outside court. I tripped down steps and along a deserted back lane between the evergreens. Reaching the water tower, a sentinel over this sadness, I come upon a doubles match. I was amazed as well as revitalized. Two short footed intense Russians playing two stringbean Americans from the Deep South.

A crowd collected. The Russian chunky bodies leaping around the court. They seemed awkward but friendly types and I wondered how it was that this naughty race had caused so much heartbreak. Then I heard the magnolia scented accents crackling out the dialogue. They were devastating these two from the East. Somehow I could bear tennis no longer. I went back through the evergreens. Past the members' lawn where they took sherry under colored umbrellas. I spied some players packed to go. I approached to ask don't you want to cry, absolutely break down and shed tears on the torn tickets in the road. And sidling near to make my heartfelt remark, I am taken aback by their flinty business man's eyes. They were soon to go to Barcelona all expenses paid.

More clapping and I know that inside centre court they're handing out the silver cups and plates. To those, who when it was match point and needed, got securely behind the cat gut and laid that chilled ball neatly at speed along the base line, out of reach. Over the tea lawn the casual labour pick up the paper cups. In the competitors' buffet, arrangements for championships elsewhere in the world are made and school girls collect autographs at the bottom of the steps. Out on the grounds the blue and the green canvas covers lie over the turf. The water tower like a lonely mausoleum standing over the empty courts. The grass worn and brown. And I make a last visit to the gents which was a day ago like a train station.

When I Bought a Bear

I went in the door with a pound. Wrapped up in the tight fist. I thought maybe you're only a kid once and never again. Mostly. And I looked over all these red bouncy things with bricks and houses and dinky toys. And I said have you got a bear. One that I can wash.

She moved with a smile and said I've got just the thing in sponge. I told her my child is desperate for some cuddly animal. And I want something that will last because we live on a boat and there's nowhere to play.

I held the furry thing with a squeeze in my hand and said how much. A guinea. I took one of those breaths that's almost the last. And sometimes I think maybe I have my share of pounds and even a little pile I keep to look at in my drawer. But a pound's a pound even in a pile. And then night time looking down on the little sleeping squealless face makes my eyes tingle with a tear and maybe a toy's not too much to ask. And I'm not a man for buying frilly flippant things. But this bear was sponge and washable and would do for years. So madam take my pound.

With it resting nestled in an arm I took the bus called twenty two. Sat on top in front looking down on the sunny crowd. Gladness on every face. Bonnets and buns swish and swinging between all the hips. And this bear can even bounce and play forever.

Through the little square with trees and fountain sprinkling in the middle and by where they have the two big guns I always feel will go bang. All the houses they brighten up to sell and coffee shops with yellow stripes of richery. In there they smile, smoke and laugh. I love them all.

At my own little corner by the river I step down and cross between the trucks to my boat bumping on the tide. My brave flag flying from the stern. In there I hear the gurgle of mother and child. Sometimes I think I'm too young to be a father but I can't go back now. Maybe there's a chop laced with garlic for dinner and later I can go out back and watch the river and bridge lit up, bulbs bobbing on the steel. I have a lot of little pleasures stowed away.

Down the gangway and I yelled I was home and had it in this bag and what should we do give it to her now. Or surprise her in the morning. How much was it. I can't tell you. How much. A guinea. O no. O yes. O dear. It washes. Is it gold. Sponge.

We rolled her round the soapy tub for a bath and put her in her own little snugly bed for bye byes with fuzzy bear. There were smiles and kicking and hugs and kissing. I sang a song about the moon and said night night little girl and bear. And all bears and bees like honey. And bears cost money.

As I do these nights, tired and full of sleep, I lay back and listened to the strange tune they play in the park across the river where they have the house of wax and fountains raging. And the barges go by booming and send the river rippling. And if a toy is a joy no price is too high to pay.

I slept that night like a bomb. With morning a red rare sun. I got up and perked the coffee on the stove. Got the butter out of my new cooling crock and laid it all over the toast and covered it all in salami. Then I went to take a look at the wind and smoke out of the stacks all over the sky. The clock over there says eight. And someday maybe I'll have a garden and room to breathe.

There were some little screams. And I didn't know what

to do first. I heard the plop and ran in. Little baby was near the window. No bear anywhere. Prayers please. It can't happen to me. Out there on the tide, two furry ears and glass eyes. I stand here watching the river rushing out to sea. One pound, one shilling.

Paddling and Persons at Putney

It takes enormous energy to tell lies. And the truth is I'm neither sad nor glad about the boat race. But it became something which was going on across the river.

After winter comes spring and then the Boat Race. All along the Thames on that day every inch is choked with people, all making a democratic racket, with drums, clapper machines and vocal cords. Oxford or Cambridge could be a sandwich but everyone's got a passion for one or the other. And a rippling roar meets the boats as they shoot up along the river and disappear around a bend.

But what is choice, if not chic, are the March afternoons of the week before. When the addicted take a No. 22 bus, a scooter or Bentley over Putney Bridge and down the Embankment past the starting marker for the University Boat Race, a granite post set with the letters U B R. Then past the curious sordid gaiety of a monstrous hotel. They say naughty naughty goes on in hotels near rivers in England but I feel sure this is an outrageous untruth. Swans float by. Along with tons of horrifying garbage. And some days, an interesting sight, when the river overflows as the tide comes up and swans merrily sail down the middle of the street with kids paddling proud kayaks.

But ahead of me now, a gathering. They stand mumchance, carelessly, effortlessly, blinking their eyes. Some with polo coats, me in my usual astrakhan and a few oddbird parsons wearing black. Except for the few upstarts who twirl mustaches and sport blazers, the ignoring of one another is rampant. I of course, merely look foreign wherever

I am, flashing, however, a rather choice English accent which when it slips has an even better one underneath. For watching oarsmen you can't do much better than that these days. So I lean against the fender behind me, a Rolls Royce of some rakish vintage. Now we are a thin but select group. And with nothing said, we are accent tested down to the last murmur.

Both Oxford and Cambridge are in their respective boathouses as the guests of the Westminster and Barclay banks. A nice background. For these banks are big and possessed of tidy sums. And from each boathouse fly two flags with a bank one on top. So with colors flowing in a gentle wind from the west, and hopefully, a sun, the moment we wait for comes. Oxford bouncing down the boathouse steps in their sneakers, having of course briefly paused and posed on the terrace. They stand in a circle in front of the open boathouse doors, with the upturned shell inside, and commence exercises. The crowd gathers close. The diminutive cox shouts commands in his elegant, elephant sized voice. They do the protracted deep-knee bend. An approving hush from the onlookers.

Out on the river now. The sleek white yacht of the BBC, television cameras fixed on a flying deck, as they race back and forth making the most interesting waves come ashore, and I suppose arranging shots. And suddenly a procession of pleasure steamers, empty and cobwebbed from winter, pass down river. The hoot of tugs, barges in tow with their skippers leaning over thick arms, smoking pipes. These pleasure steamers take up the fantastic rear of the race. Jammed with graduates of all kinds, including the under ones as well as a few risqué types who may have utterly failed at college and now feebly flair forth on boat race day. One jolly bunch altogether.

There is an aesthetic difference, and perhaps even more than that, between Oxford and Cambridge. The latter are more reserved, thinner in the face, and do not have the ruddy complexions of Oxford. And they are mostly last for practice. They arrive in their charabanc just as Oxford are moving out in the stream and set off for Hammersmith Bridge, a mile and a half away. The crowd has thinned somewhat then but I feel those who are left are more sedate. There are always a few young women in the crowd. One usually long, lank and blonde. Unlike me, she leans against the dazzle of a Mercedes Benz, blonde legs crossed, blonde voice saying, I suppose, in the blonde brain, 'I am blonde, I will, after the race, marry a banker.'

Two bankers approach. Bowler hatted and flat bellied, that's how I know them. They pause nearby for some back slapping. The blows are delivered with the palm and heel of the hand to the small of the back. The idea is to produce coughing and in some cases retching, depending upon the respective ages of the slapper and slapped. And now Cambridge come out of their boathouse, four on each side of the glistening shell. The cox leading them, his casual finger guiding them down to the water's edge. A loud command and the boat goes up, over and gently in the water. Charging back up the slipway, they return with the oars, slip out of shoes and into the boat. Carefully, one by one.

Meanwhile there is a delicious little performance. A chosen group stepping carefully down the slip and climbing into a pink railed gondola. Big mufflers round the throats, dressed in lambskin, coonskin, and always one tasty woman preening in the latest. There may be of course, the odd escaped lunatic or convict here but they are indistinguishable from ordinary folk due to their extreme good manners and pleasant smiling faces. Especially since they would be mixed among a few Old Blues, stampeding toward the gondola, who can look like nothing on earth. Some are ninety years old. With heart pumps, they say, as good as ever. All bundled up like bears. The squeaking ancient legs are lifted up and over the pink rails, pillows carefully placed to receive bottoms.

And whoops. This happened once. An Old Blue slips a leg into the drink. You may think there was no laughter. But the crowd suddenly, admittedly only for an instant, became a howling mob. I thought of Tyburn Hill and the hangings. And roared myself but inwardly of course, using the pursed lips as a disguise. The dunked Old Blue let out a not unbecoming seal bark. They dragged him out of the swirling grey water by the armpits. He swan flapped around the gondola. The rugs were rushed to him. The gondola rocked disastrously. And it nearly happened. Just what you're thinking. The women screamed. But the Old Blue, true to school, tie and that oar he once held, shouted his advice over the howls of horror, 'Save the women and children first, leave the men till later.'

And so the launch gets filled. The Oxford coach up front, dark blue cap on head, megaphone at his mouth and sprig of violets in his buttonhole. The helmsman manoeuvring in the strong tide. On the slip the crew step into the boat, fit in their oars and wait. A photographer taking pictures. Sets of teeth sparkle everywhere. The real and the false. And the shell with eight eager oarsmen is pushed gently out into the tide. A few well modulated instructions float across the water from the coach. The cox sets his chin evenly, draws wind into his lungs and shouts, 'Off scarves.' Out come the red pouches and in go the scarves and all is tucked neatly back under the sliding seats. Another command, 'Come forward.' And the crew lean into their oars, blades back. And then, 'Are you ready.' Great silence everywhere and finally, 'Paddle.' And the slender shell with eight flashing splashes leaps away on the lead colored Thames.

Now watch them paddle with their long slow stroke to turn widely below Putney Bridge, then with the tide pouring behind them, paddle back up to be grabbed by the stake boats. Down river, the armada of launches, speedboats and yachts greedily anticipate. Light and dark blue flags wave and wag madly from bridge, window and shore. And then silence. They wait. And suddenly they're off. Two slim insects catching eight claws on the water. Followed by this frenzied flotilla, spreading the river in white waves with cheers and gay scarves flying. And out of one mountainous coat, I see an Old Blue, jaw set like the prow of a ship, eyes glued and feverish on this brief spectacle that starts all over again next spring.

In My Peach Shoes

She was dressed in the best she had. I went to meet her going on the long highway. I heard from sources she was tickled pink to go out with me. Naturally I felt big time. I was going straight north. Saw the police parked all fat in blue waiting for speeders. They looked at me from behind the sunglasses. You've never seen such bellies in blue. I looked back with that air I've got, that I know somebody who knows somebody who's something and you better watch out. It made no impression and I kept going north on the bright whistling concrete.

Big tents spread out in the trees on every side. I think I saw banners and bass drums. And there she was, covered with her haystack hair. And I wiggled my toes. I have always paid peculiar attention to shoes. And these peach ones I was wearing made me feel smooth. With a neat breath I put an inch extra on my chest and smiled. And she smiled. The smile she used as a child. What a real mouth and large teeth, her wide straw hat over her straw hair. And a worried frown as she peered at my shoes.

The restaurant with its flat roof and factory windows. And we walked down and down to it. My arm held for hers. To the white covered table in the sunken garden. She in her lacy white dress as the waiters went to and fro. This late high sunned afternoon. When all the deep grass is white and warm. And deep enough to hide. Perhaps my shoes. With their peach I was proud of.

But when we sat on the chairs that were iron and filigree and the table tin with holes. Doubts about my taste were evident. I could only go sad and touch the silver salt and pepper things and pretend that I was starting a fashion. Didn't she know peach was really the snazz. No. She did not know. I walked away and left her there.

I went up the wide steps from this old but lavish eatery. The waiters worrying in and out their kitchen door. The head man looking at me depart and down his nose towards my tootsies. All the others had come clothed in furs and lace, women in white, men in black with employees hurrying round them everywhere.

And she sat all alone waiting for me to come back. With her pinkly colored nail she touched the table things one by one. Nothing came for her to eat. That's embarrassing in a restaurant. She pitied my bad taste. And she's not getting anything to taste at all. I flew the banner of a hero in my heart but outside where others could see me I was a heel.

Watching through the window. Waiters passing out the peach melba. Trays and trays of clotted cream. Yummy. She sits silent. The head man comes and whispers. Now she cries quietly. Waiters come take the things away. She raises her head to look. I hope for me. Her tan face wet. And the others are picking up their lavish furs around their smooth shoulders and bowed to and smiled upon they're gone.

The sun comes down. I think of places like roads of ash and poison ivy patches. To which I am immune. And she's not. Now the employees come and take the table and lift down the flowers from the walls. And say sorry Miss but we can't help it, we've got to take your chair. She stood brown clenched hands to her eyes.

I got up from position. Slipped off the shoes, socks too, white with monogram. I froze my smile of the potentate across my appearance. And with the slow step I moved through doors down and down into the midst of this preposterous eatery. I raised my voice. They saw the diamonds sparkling on my toes. My total demeanour was disdain. Like flashes they brought the eating instruments. Her eyes wide with horror drew narrow with love. And after the melba I presented a foot. I said quietly. The color of this too, is peach.

When I Brought the News

I thought I was going to be a millionaire. With moroccan bound books for looks everywhere. And even a drive that went for a mile through the trees and little lakes and lilies. So in my best serious face I stood in line for the job and told the nervous man I'd work very hard.

Every afternoon loaded down I set off on the outskirts of town folding papers with a sleight of hand and flicking them across the grey porches. And even in an open window for a laugh which I thought I needed. And as I proceeded along this frontier road picking berries grapes and peaches I said hi to the rival newspaper boy and told him he was underpaid and you'll never make the money I've made. But it was a lie.

Because Friday I collected and most said come back tomorrow and I objected but turned my sad face away and mumbled it was only a dime. And you'd think it was a crime every time I rang a doorbell and even those with chimes and added up the weeks they owed. In there they sit warm and reading, with smells of steak and pizza pie. Out here lips chapped with frost I might die, dancing on my cold toes. There's only so much I can stand, you savage hearts.

But I was glad at times along here in sun on these quiet roads where some buildings were built in the sky out of trees and near the river. The green the grass the cliffs and hills and bridges bent over the trains. Cool summer halls to click heels and spin down the stairs on my educated wrist.

Noisy with the news. And deep in my own unsavage heart I loved nothing better than delivery.

And Saturdays in Autumn afternoon kicking through the leaves I came to ring the bell and knock on the door and say I beg you pay me please. And the heads with after lunch eyes came out too beaten to refuse. In my little book I marked them paid and with some quiet charm of mine I tried to make them feel it was not the end of the world. And maybe there would be a new woman's page soon. Or a competition for a prize.

But some heartless called me liar and lingerer. Napping under trees, banging on doors and a whistler in halls. I whispered something about freedom and they shouted don't come back no more and slammed the door. I walked away with young tears melting with despair. They'd all be sorry when they found me Christmas Eve shoeless and starved, dead in the snow.

And weeks went by till one Sunday dawn in black winter I brought my pencil. I wrote across the front page HOW DOES IT FEEL TO CHEAT A CHILD. And tucked the paper carefully in the door. Monday creeping through the streets I saw the raging faces watching from windows everywhere and a man on a porch shaking a fist which he said would break my head. And fearful but forceful I told him drop dead. And ran.

I prayed for spring when I could sing once more and steal the cooling cooky from a window sill. With the sun such a fat red thing up in the sky. And count my blessings instead of money. But things were sad instead of sunny when Mr Brown screeched up in his sporty car. I wore my slack jaw. He wagged a finger, confound you D, the News is deluged with complaints, your public relations are a scandal, the customers claim you're a nuisance and a vandal and did you write how does it feel to cheat a child? I did. Confound you D, don't you know the customer is always right? Come along with me and apologise. I said no. He said so, you're fired.

Never to bring the news again. Or trap a customer on the street or write my editorial across the front page. A failed millionaire with no moroccan bound books for looks anywhere.

Franz F

He lived in Elderberry Street, in the West End of Boston, and had a shop front with a cold water flat behind. In the basement of the building a man made wine and the fermented smell came up between the floor boards. The kitchen was misshapen, small and dark and whenever Franz turned on the light a lot of roaches would scurry over the sink and disappear in the wall.

The little living room had a built in couch on which Franz slept. Some bookcases around the wall and in a farther tiny room there was another bed. Rattan shades on all the windows to keep out eyes passing in the alley. A big woolly rug on the floor. This was a lonely outpost. Except for the loud fights that went on in the rest of the building and sometimes on both sides of the street.

At six any morning when he could not sleep, Franz stood in the shadow of his doorway to listen to the alarm clocks going off up and down the street, the ringing of these sad timepieces escaping out the open windows. Then taking a shower, and at eight fifty every morning, Monday to Friday, he put particulars in his briefcase, cornflakes inside him, and set off.

Elderberry a narrow street with one or two grotesque trees arching and sneaking their branches between the houses. Empty flats to rent with the price written in white grease on the windows. Some buildings had fallen down and had become vacant lots where cars were parked. Franz F walking toward the river, slinging his briefcase ahead of him, sweeping his free arm across his face at the clouds of flies blossoming off the garbage as he passed. By the river there was a breeze, a brightness of water, and an early-morning green.

Sometimes he went down behind the hospital past a red brick wall with a pair of big dark doors. If these were open, there was an empty trolley waiting by the steps. And certain times a black van from a funeral parlor would pull out, a man preceding it to warn traffic in the narrow street. Above these large doors were windows Franz could see into from the other side of the road. Shelves around the wall of a large room, rows of bottles and bottles. This is how we went one day.

The hospital extended to the river. And here were grass, trees, and the building's high balconies and curtained windows. Someone sitting in a wheelchair reading. And outside this entrance were always parked several long expensive cars. It gave one heart. Inside, a bright reception desk in the gleaming hall. And elderly women with canes and furs were helped up the steps by their chauffeurs.

On the hottest days there was always freshness here along the river. Young maple trees spreading over the paths. At night the factory buildings across the water shone bright neon lights and rippled and flickered. Saturdays and Sundays the sailboats were out. White one winged butter-flies.

Past the hospital was the jail. Always a little difficult to decide which place would be better to be, hospital or jail. But upon serious consideration of this problem, Franz chose the jail. At least it was near the river and within a stone's throw of Charles Street Station. Nice to know that if you did make it over the wall you were near public transport.

Climbing the steps to the station platform, Franz was a rigid figure, a lonely one in his Victorian suiting. In the train he always offered his seat to a woman. Doing so evoked a feeling that all was well with the world. Often there were tall horse faced girls travelling, who crossed legs largely lean and read books in their laps. If Franz was early for work he went for coffee in Harvard Square. This pleasant time of day, when the college buildings were coming awake with the summery flap of blue sneakers along the pavement. A tremendous change to come out of the enclosed darkness of Elderberry Street to these open spacious buildings. To see the bright smiling teeth of students. His train pulling into this last stop, a new atmosphere in the air. White clean walls of the tunnel. The magazine kiosk. Even the weighing and gum machines had a clean magic about them. And here he weighed one hundred and seventy one pounds and bought his gum.

Franz F worked in a building just off the Square. It had the feeling of a library. There was a reception desk where a young blond woman, her hair tightly back in a bun, nodded her head to him as he came in. He doffed his cap, gave a slight bow, just so. A little frightened that she thought him pretentious. And his clothes a little too old worldly to be honest. He hoped as he rambled by each morning that she might ask him a question because he looked so intelligent. But her face was always neither sad nor glad and her name was Lydia.

Her legs he knew by heart. Neat muscles knotting over long ankles and toes slightly pigeon. In the outside corner of each eye she had put a dark pencil line that gave her face a touch of Chinese beauty. Her silence made him feel she was aloof and slightly censuring. But passing each morning, he felt he wasn't doing too badly.

Climbing up the stairs to his room where two wide windows overlooked the street and opening his briefcase on the long board table. His hands looked such trembling hooks, freckled, tired and grey. This day was like all the rest and might be like all his future. In going to the window, raising it wide, putting elbows on the sill and looking down at the street and the tailor shop across, there was an iota of hope.

All through one's life there were the myriad days at school while outside was summertime under the skies.

As the mornings grew toward noon, messengers brought sheets of yellow paper with many statistics. He went down line after line with his pencil, checking those which were related and made a list. From this list other lists would be made. And from these, in another room at the top of the building, people who had higher positions would come to a conclusion.

This office was a lonely life. Two or three infrequent acquaintances might stop by, peek through the door, and chat for a minute. There was a feeling, reading these faces, that they were saying, come on and fight. But getting the gimlet eye, they retreated, making a wisecrack, and were off down the hall to more influential people. The uncomfortable feeling descending on Franz that they were going to intrigue him out of his job.

There were bigger problems than losing one's job. Franz had for many years been interested in having an affair with a woman. One of those things where you like me and I like you. Things would start bravely enough. His shirt, underwear, and seersucker had been oven fresh for those light-blue evenings. The girl tall, fragrant, and socially registered perhaps. And to have his invitation accepted was undermining. He thought there was a secret with women, a combination that unlocked the chastity. That when you phoned to ask them to come to the Bach quartet, you sent a flower that afternoon. And often then, calling at her house, the bloom pinned to her dress hung wilted on its stem, a faded three-dollar overture.

On these dates he took a taxi drive with the girl along the grassy banks of the Charles. Sitting stiffly upright, designating points of interest. And amazed at the nice looking clothes the girl had on. So many attempts in his life to arrange a scene of seduction. Cutting family ties, finding the privacy of one's own quarters, roach ridden as they were.

No friends who might pay a call casually and thus wreck a wrestle. But his suggestion for coffee after the concert met with a request to be taken home. The dutiful delivery, walking to their front doors, doffing hat, bowing, saying good night. The door closing, walking away, almost feeling her sigh of relief on the back of his neck.

On these nights, the shop in Elderberry Street became a pit of despair. Nothing to lighten the burden of darkness. Maybe run the shower, chase the roaches. Go out past a bar, think of having a drink, see the smoke and the sour menacing men inside and instead buy a quart of beer from the corner store. The man shortchanging him two cents without fail. And they would go through the usual routine of, oh sorry, and a reluctant two pennies would be dropped one at a time into his upward palm.

Saturday mornings after these terrible Fridays, Franz with shirt and tie would saunter toward the river, walking along past the jail to buy a New York Times at the drugstore. Along Charles Street, past the soothing brick, where inside there must be bliss to make the outside look so mellow. Behind the screened windows tall horse faced women whispering out of the shadows to husbands, darling, come and kiss me. Were it he, he would likely slip and break his neck rushing across the polished floor to her mouth.

And this Saturday morning, a balmy breeze dipping in his hair, Franz made for the Public Garden, paper folded under his arm. An oasis of gigantic trees. Spindle shanked women anciently wrapped in Manx rugs reading with magnifying glasses on the benches. The swan boats quietly churning from pond to pond under the bridges.

Today all the benches were taken and Franz made for the circular one around the tree. Two people go by, each with a bulldog. A nannie pushing twins in a baby carriage. Sitting down, crossing his legs, tugging up socks, Franz opened to the obituaries. He read the prominent deads. Not like the hot days in Elderberry Street, where you could see the bald pate of the undertaker gleaming from the upper half of his window as he worked. These deads in the paper did not die in vain.

Franz heard the words, which came from the other side of the tree. He looked up and then back at his paper. He heard the words again and turned around. A girl's foot and ankle jigging up and down, and he went back to his paper. Once more he heard the words and there was a sizzling in his stomach. They were simple ancient words almost without meaning, do you have a match.

Leaning around the tree, Franz said to what he could see of this person, are you talking to me. And she said, yes, well, I think so. Do you have a match. Franz thought that if he did not have a match he would get up and run as fast as he could to the drugstore on the corner of Charles and Beacon Streets, and there get a match and run back with it already lit, holding his hand before the flame. The utter panic of this thought hit Franz and he laughed outright. The girl leaned forward and said, what's the matter. Franz said it was something in his paper. And she said, well, do you have a match.

Grimness spread on Franz's lips. Hands came up to his eyes like cups to catch the tears. He had no match. His voice disappeared as well. The thought of actually making a run for the drugstore was too much. Like all women he had terrorized previously, this one too, would be gone by the time he got back. The hurried trip for the matches he might pass off as a gesture, a new knighthood. Alas, she would think it lunacy. Here he was, rooted to the spot, dying on each heartbeat.

Sitting, his newspaper clutched in one hand, knees wide apart and feet so flat upon the path. Saturday, the hour before lunch. My God, what to say to the other side of the tree. There had been school days like this when teachers sent questions thudding on some dream. And you sat mumchance.

And her voice once more, I'm sorry if I bothered you. He heard her getting up. A foot crushing a cinder. And Franz said, don't go away.

In that public garden Franz sat talking out toward Arlington Street as she talked in the direction of Boylston. An open air confessional. His resonance increasing as the conversation went on. She said she came from the other end of earth. This statement a little scalding for Franz. But the place was New Zealand and he had heard of it before. Another item was, she was married to a Bostonian. He had heard of this too.

She said she did not like America and was sorry she ever came. Her husband was a bore. So Franz told her of the delights of Boston. Beacon Hill, the red brick pavements, T Wharf, and the quiet seclusion of life. And she said that North Station waiting for trains had been enough of Boston for her.

She got up and came to look at him around the other side of the tree. She was smiling at the foolish situation. She lived in Beaver Place. She said she had to meet someone but that he was interesting. Franz thought, O my God, when will the lies begin. And he walked her to the edge of the park, waving to her when she stopped and looked back from the corner of Beacon and Arlington. He had her telephone number. She told him to ring, perhaps next week.

One Sunday, Franz came again to the Public Garden. Sat where he'd been sitting and relived the encounter. Remembering all the pebbles and each leaf of every weed. In joyous confusion he even bowed to one of the old ladies in her Manx rug and she raised an eye brow, what was left of it.

He had scrubbed out his entire flat. And then tramped across Boston City. Through Scollay Square, down State Street, into the thick life of the markets. Waiting to phone her. To invite her up his decrepit street, by his begrimed store window, in the dust of which kids had written, if you're so smart why aren't you rich. Young kids have such clear minds.

And if she came and when she came would she get cold feet as she neared, looking for his address. Get her to go by the library and along the worn dignity of Blossom Street. He could say something at the door, a verbal gallantry. The telephone was polished and placed just outside the kitchen on his octagonal table and perhaps would give dash to these digs.

All this figured out on Sunday. A day when Franz finally sat for hours on the end of T Wharf staring out across Boston harbor. The sights and sounds of when all this was low scrubland, peopled by strange singular Indians. And a truck driver had come up to him and said, this ain't nothing compared to that harbor they got in Frisco. I just finished driving from there.

And Monday through the routine, except for an extra bun and coffee in the morning. The purchase of a new shirt from the tailor across the street at lunchtime, holding it like a book as he passed the receptionist. And that evening back in Elderberry Street, after a shower and half an hour's deliberation, the final desperate writing out the words on a sheet of paper and pinning it to the wall above the phone. Franz dialled her number.

Another girl had to fetch her. A lot of voices in the background. All the people he knew were so brave on the telephone. She said hello and he asked her through his fumbling voice would she come and have a coffee at his apartment. Silence. He said hello. She said hello. He said, what about it. She said no, she didn't think she could. He said, as the emptiness got bigger, oh, you're still listening. You haven't hung up yet. And she said, no, I haven't hung up. Is that all you've got to say. Franz said, no, I've got more. And she said, well, I can't wait all night. And then he said, would you like to see a play. She said, what. Franz said, I don't know, just a play. And she said, what a funny thing to ask me to. I'm sorry but I've got to go now, goodbye.

Franz gently hung up the phone. Standing in his dark shop where once they sold vegetables. He put his hand up to his brow and wiped away the dripping sweat. He closed his arms around his chest and held himself as he wept.

For a whole week Franz spoke to no one. Taking his lunchtime sandwiches to the steps of Widener Library, he publicly tore at the crusts. He kept the door of his office closed and his head bent over the yellow sheets. In the evenings, unable to face the cloistered loneliness of Elderberry Street, he walked the streets of Cambridge. And one night, passing a straightbacked little crowd, he stopped and followed them and bought a ticket to a play.

Teeth tightly clenched in his mouth as he came to work next morning, eyes ahead, and the receptionist stopped him dead in his tracks. She said, hey. And he turned and she came out from behind her counter and told him she had sat behind him last night at the Poet's Theatre. Wearing a hard distant look and nodding his head, he went his way up the stairs and left her standing there.

In the late night in Elderberry Street, Franz lay head on pillow staring at the sounds of feet as they walked on the ceiling above. He avoided the back end of the hospital these days and once he went swimming in the pool at the end of the street. But all were jaws of more loneliness. He had become a conversation piece on the steps of Widener Library.

And then one afternoon, cap square on head, eyes bearing zero, he passed across the reception hall to go home. The receptionist stepped out in front of him and said, God damn it, you're rude. Franz blinked, stepped back, and tried to make it around her. She said, yes, you're God damned rude, and who the hell wants to speak to you anyhow. Franz said, you do, but nobody else does.

That night, after sitting head in hands in the tall reading

room of the library off Blossom Street, Franz thought he might turn on the gas and block up his doors and windows. But it would be weeks before they'd find him, and the indignity was too much. He thought of giving up his job. Before, he had always waited until he was fired. Perhaps he could go back to Europe. Instead, he went to the local bakery, down the steps, smelling the moist dough, crusts baking, and this Italian gentleman who always asked him questions.

And tonight this baker said, you know, mister, you always look important to me, and you never say a thing. Aren't you ever going to tell me what you are. Franz said, yes, tonight I'll tell you. I'm a comma. Franz, gathering the two long loaves in his arms, stepped up the steps, and the Italian gentleman shouted after him, hey, you're a comedian.

Franz chopped up a mound of garlic and made a paste with butter. Slathering the long loaves, he put them in the oven. This lonely act of defiance. Reek tomorrow on the train. Pass by Lydia. Such an unlikely name. Perhaps she would tell him he was not only rude but reeking.

Lights out now in Elderberry Street. Twelve o'clock, when at last the voices stop squabbling out the windows in the alley. A quick roach kill and spash of water on the face. To lie back under the sheet and try to close the eyes. A bleary voice entering the alley. A woman with a customer. Franz still on his couch. Hearing her rap on his window. Hey, you in there, why don't you ever talk. Too good for us around here. What are you anyway. Franz said from his cloister, I'm a comedian.

Peals of laughter as she pulled herself up the back stairs, tugging her customer, shouting, did you hear what he said, that bastard in seersucker. He says he's a comedian. What a laugh. He's queer, that's what he is. Never seen him with a woman. You hear me, you God damn bastards in the rest of this house. Think you're too good for me. He's a queer.

In sleep there was an Autumn afternoon in Vermont, with all the woods red red gold. Tennis players and one was Lydia. She took his hand and said, not tonight. And he tiptoed and tiptoed to her door, rapping lightly as she said, you mustn't, you mustn't. Then as he slept she came and laid herself upon him, a smell of musk from her breasts. Waking now, a corner of swift blue high out beyond the alley in Elderberry Street, Franz begged the dream to come back.

All the way to work, he planned it. Walk up to Lydia, brief bow, and say, I want to apologise for my inexcusable rudeness the other day, and also for smelling of garlic this morning. Then spin on the heel and go up the stairs. But entering the open door, Franz passed her by, with a rigid fearful heart. Reaching his room, the bubbling of the water cooler outside the door, he silently pounded his fists on his table.

Each morning he had it planned, the mountain growing bigger and more impossible to climb. When suddenly she said, I don't know why I'm telling you this, but there's a plot to intrigue you out of your job.

As his knees buckled and his face went ashen, Franz sent whispers into his mind saying over and over, play it cool, play it cool. To Lydia he said, why are you telling me this. She said, because you've got no one to help you. Franz said, thanks, and so that she wouldn't notice the moisture in his eyes he turned and went up the stairs.

This time always came. Like clockwork. Just when his life ticked temperately, they got together to oust him. Not because he had mixed the statistics. Or infracted a rule. But because he came to work neither late nor soon, that he bowed gently, dressed in his own fashion and regarded life with his gimlet eye. He did what they told him. Sometimes they will kill you for that.

But more than the token terror of dismissal was the curiosity of a woman with fine bones to her face and a gracious body, helping him. She was married and had nothing to fear. Each afternoon, a cartridge bag slung from her shoulder, she stepped up on the electric car and disappeared along Mount Auburn Street away under the trees of Cambridge. To go behind hedges and into a big white house because he had followed her one afternoon.

It seemed they had made peace. For she smiled once and even licked her lips as he smiled back. He could not engage in the battle to save himself because it was just one army after one man. Yours truly. And in these cases one could only skiddoo.

On a Thursday, Franz F packed up. Dusted and polished his office and took down his poem.

> When the going
> Is too good
> To be true
> Reverse course
> And beat it.

It was a long trip back to Elderberry Street. And inside this address Franz let the roaches run wild. Friday morning he went down the street and straight across to the swimming pool where he clonked into the meter one penny. For an hour he lived like a seal. Some of the kids wanted to know why he wasn't working. Their insolence was amusing.

A letter arrived. His resignation was accepted and herewith two weeks' salary. Franz popped this blue green check back in an envelope and returned it to that sunny building off Harvard Square. He took a sheet of paper and put down another poem. This he stuck over the sink.

> When you've
> Beat it
> And the going
> Is too desperate
> To be true
> Forge on.

Over the weekend Franz bought beer and let the man cheat him of the two cents. But as he turned out of the store, the man called him back and said, hey, what's the matter. You upset or something. Franz said, no. The man said, don't you know I'm robbing you two cents. Franz said, yes. The man said, I can't help it, it's a habit.

For twenty five cents on Tuesday Franz bought a pound of kidneys. And was frying these in olive oil. A balanced diet for the siege. And standing on a chair fanning smoke out the window, there came a knock on his door. On the steps handing him an envelope was Lydia.

She said, I have this for you. Franz took it and said, thanks. She said, so this is where you live. He said, yes. And she said, well aren't you going to ask me in. Franz saw eyes and faces hanging out the windows. This was news for Elderberry Street. He said, sure, come in if you want.

Franz directed her through the smoke. In the sitting room she sat on his bed. She said, you're such a funny and silly person, you're going to lose all the way through life. Why didn't you put up a fight. They thought they could fire you only because you ate your lunch on the steps of Widener Library. And then to send the check back was so silly.

In the hour evaporating away they had tea. Franz brought out the Peek Frean biscuits. Made a rose of them on a plate. She said, something seemed to have happened to you a while back. Suddenly you stopped talking to everybody. You were so grim. Franz said yes, he was grim. She said, that's why I wanted to make friends with you, and you just snubbed me. Franz said that was true, he had snubbed her. And Lydia had another Peek Frean and rising, said she had to go.

Franz led her sadly into the kitchen. He pulled the light cord and Lydia stopped in the dark. Franz said, I don't want you to see the roaches. She said, I don't mind what I see. And as Franz put his arms around her she whispered, you mustn't, you mustn't. Franz said, you've said that to me before, and he pressed his lips on the scent behind her ear. And she said will you be here next Saturday afternoon. I'll come at three thirty.

Franz took the envelope and check and burned them over the stove. He took a pail of water and washed the store window. The kids crowded around, hey, what's a matter, mister. You trying to make your place look good. Franz rolled a nickel down the street, quietly relishing as the kids wrestled in the gutter.

Each morning rising, beating fists on chest, touching toes, breathing God's air. Tearing open the front door and smiling out into the street. Buy the paper and read it over a coffee and crumb cake in Charles Street. And then militantly to the Public Garden, where there was half an hour's revenge on the circular bench around the tree.

Lydia was light haired. And she would walk pigeon toed, her body curved in, passing by all the cellar entrances, dark alleys and broken windows and knock on his door. And at twenty past three on this Saturday Franz had changed his underwear twice in the last hour. The weather report was cool. And the world light blue. And his hands trembling. This was a lonely station. A chair by the telephone, eyes glued on the door.

And the phone rang. Picking up this black talking instrument Franz heard a nearby muffled voice that said, this is Lydia's husband, and I've got my gun and I'm coming round to shoot you.

The telephone fell out of Franz's hand and lay on the floor making a gurgling sound. The little words of his office poem. When the going is too good to be true.

Franz got up and unlocked the door, leaving it slightly ajar. He returned to his chair, having made his decision. The afternoon was deep red. Save him the trouble of knocking. And now after all these years it would be a curious justice that would put him down. Franz sitting slumped forward facing the door, hanging his head and hands. Perhaps he would have the dignity of being shot by a college graduate.

As the door opened Franz F closed his eyes and turning his head aside, raised his hands to block the bullets. The steps came near and a hand touched him on the hair and Lydia said, oh my God I phoned you as a joke.

A Fraternal Fraud

For the purpose of power or laughs or almost anything, I once made up a fraternity. Had a meeting every week and I was brother master and the rest were brothers. My best friend Jimmy, treasurer. To get in took six months. Pledges had to wear a black tie, carry a demerit book, and obey all orders from brothers. Also pay fifteen dollars which I counted with the treasurer. We were partial to rich boys.

And magic secret ceremonies like the ritual of the worms. Barefoot pledges step blindfolded into a pan of wet spaghetti. There is a cry called a screech.

For sixty bucks we got a station wagon and put Omega Omega Omega on the sides. Then parked it in an alley where it got stuck between the walls. Everyone bragging how they could drive. I'll get it out, just watch me. Won a medal for this and my father's got one too, so watch me. And we watched. It wedged tighter and tighter, tyres burning down to the tubes. We had to give up. I gave orders from the back seat to abandon ship and clear the decks generally. And couldn't go out the doors. In the end we escaped through the roof.

Initiation fees coming in left and right and centre. Capital was considerable. Greed general. I got crazy for power. Touched by wildness. And the hammer of discipline.

'Say pledge I don't like the way you wear your face when you look at me.'

'Gee brother, sir, I didn't mean anything. I guess my mouth just slipped.'

'Give me your demerit book, pledge, that's two demerits, you know what ten means?'

'Yes sir, blackball.'

'Well watch it then. From now on you wear your face with humility or better make that saint like. Get me? And chew this.'

'But that's garlic, gee.'

'You hear what I said.'

'But what am I going to do during the rush hour they'll all look at me.'

'Grind it. With the back teeth.'

'Holy mackerel this burns brother master.'

'Don't be chicken.'

After meetings, fights on the backs of pledges on front lawns. For body building. Get bored.

'O.K. pledge go over to that house and ask them if they want to buy a mountain.'

'Gee brother supposing a man comes to the door and slugs me.'

'Look pledge, if Omega Omega Omega doesn't mean that much to you that you wouldn't take a few slugs in the teeth I'd just as soon blackball you right now on the spot. No place for yellowness in this fraternity. Tell them there's gold.'

'What if he hits me before I open my mouth.'

'Get over there fast or I'll tell you to go without your pants.'

'Gee don't. Sir. I'm going right now.'

'That's better. Build up your nerve. And wipe off the hang-dog look. If he gets tough start yelling maybe your neighbours ought to know what a cheapskate lives next door. If he asks where the mountain is tell him East Geek. Then you can run. I'll be right behind that hedge listening. Make it good.'

Behind the hedge. The bell ringing to the tune of the 'Bells of Saint Mary.' Maybe they're not such bad people having a song like that attached to the bell. Feet. Heavy ones. Whoops. Must stick to my post. Lose face to retreat. Taking off the burglar latch. He's big.

'Good evening sir. I'm from Omega Omega Omega . . .'

'We don't want to buy nothing.'

'But . . .'

'Say you deaf. I don't want to buy nothing that's English ain't it.'

'But there's gold in this mountain.'

'What mountain, what are you crazy or something?'

'I'd like to talk it over with your wife.'

'Oh you would, would you.'

'And it's a bargain only open for a week to people in this high class area who are big time and really out for a kill.'

'What do you take me for. I'll give you just five seconds to get off this porch.'

'It's in East Geek you big jerk.'

I thought maybe the range was a little close for the last remark. But the pledge went so fast that I stood up watching him. Until I felt a hand closing on an outer garment and I knew it was time to leave. Too.

I renamed this pledge the Streak and kept him near for messages. The months went by.

'Well how does it feel to have your time nearly up, Streak.'

'Gee brother, I'm a little tired of being pushed around. None of you had to pledge like us. And all that money you collect. Sir.'

'Look me right in the eye pledge. What do you see there. Straight in. Now what do you see.'

'Honesty.'

'O.K. Remember that.'

I was sitting in the big brother master's chair, legs crossed drinking beer with potato chips, tempted to get the pledge to open and close my jaws for me, dreaming of a dance with a fountain and aeroplanes landing on the lawn. Who's that. Oh just an Omega brother arriving. Impress the Streak.

Something wistful about him and believing. I think he looks up to me.

The letter came the morning of the Friday meeting. I told them to get ready for a grand council and something else as well. The meeting was in my house and I ordered a barrel of beer to wash some guilt away. I told everybody to take a seat.

'O.K. look, this is how it is. You've all been through quite a lot and you'll probably think you've been taken for a ride.'

The Streak came half way to his feet out of the chair.

'Take it easy. Nothing is ever as bad as it seems, it's always worse. I started this fraternity in good faith and was freely voted brother master and Jimmy treasurer. You'll notice Jim's not with us tonight. But he sent me a letter this morning and as a result the brothers and I have decided to disband and desist from further activity. This is what it says:

'Dear Brothers,

I went to a nightclub and got carried away with being a big wheel and was stuck for the bill which forced me to delve into the funds of Omega Omega Omega which I happened to have on me at the time. And there is not much change. Forgive me.

My cousin has invited me to Wyoming where I think I am lost forever in Yellowstone National Park.

Yours on vacation
or even longer,
Brother Treasurer.'

There were tears in the Streak's eyes.

Pins and Medals

Sitting back here with flowers on the curtains, cologne in the air and tinkling music with all the comfort.

My first real girl friend I met not far from here by saying hello and she looked in my face for signs of disrespect. In her brown sweater and skirt and all I wanted was to know her to go for a walk up and down the paths around the school. Where spruce trees grew in their blue tips to touch the windows and there were little hills and mountains for miles around and lakes clear and magic. And I'll never forget her or when she touched me on the shoulder asking for company to come with her for cake and cola. I said sure. In her house I sat on the edge of my seat while she brought it in. She stood in the middle of the floor and yawned. I put my mouth deep in the chocolate cake, cream and soft eating. Otherwise I was shy worrying whether I said what she wanted.

I whistled going home that afternoon and jumped up to sit on a mailcart thinking of her looks and waiting for the train. And later in our little nipping at love I asked her with her handkerchief twisting in her hands to come to a dance. And arrived that evening in cool late spring, a bright tie to make my suit feel new. She was dressed in blue with pleats round her skirt a sort of endless thing I thought, her legs rich round and seventeen. With two dollars and a bath and my feelings tied up inside me we stepped out from the shaky car of a friend saying hello to all the others under the maple trees. Down steps between palms to where the band was playing. I danced better than ever before. She was looking up at my face and sometimes putting hers on my shoulder. While they dripped candle wax to make funny bumps I tried to be talkative and tell her what I wanted to mean. When the rest went to a bar for drinks we sat alone in the back of the car waiting till she took a cigarette, lit it and threw it away so that we were kissing.

I never kissed anyone like her before except just once quickly somewhere and the next day we rushed back to her house hand in hand stopping only for six cola for the cake. By days we saw each other in history class and lunchtime went to have milk and crushed egg sitting on the grass. I threw my feet up carelessly anywhere while biting my bread saying I failed everything last month but didn't care. She said she wanted some sort of ring or pin of mine to wear. I gave her a medal I won throwing the weight. I was afraid to ask her for something. She showed me how nice my medal looked hanging around her tan neck. And going back through the breezy green corridors to class she said she couldn't let me have her sorority pin because it was too expensive. I went to physics where the teacher was always doing tricks like making things jump or go the other way. He called me sunshine boy because I sat by the window with my shoes off and I thought that when he made these explosions and sent stuff flying round the room we were just supposed to get a good laugh. I didn't hear him when he said it was magnetism and the atom.

One day as I stood in the sun outside school she came up to me and said she couldn't go out with me or see me Sunday because she'd been asked up to Yale for the weekend. So I said well I better have my medal back then. She said if you feel that way all right. She put her head up and bouncing all the brown curls of her hair, walked away.

On my way here tonight when I got off the train to get the bus I saw her waiting with her hands folded on her diaphragm which went out like a shelf over her pregnancy. I was so changed that when I stuck my face where I was sure she could see it she just looked and that was all. Standing there in the chill near the cemetery the bus came. I thought watching the tall white tombs go by and she waddling through her motherhood that it was a pity I could not have come one night to her bed during the dark of these last few years.

It Was My Chimes

Naturally I laughed. My tailor said Mr D have you had the suit cleaned. I said no. He said don't, the material is a distinct liability, so watch it. So I said I was watching. He said don't sit down in it, and walk with a clean stride, you don't want it to crease.

When gay eyes examine me closely I want them to see the gold thread in the garment. So when we went to eat in the roof garden I threw my careless hand in the night air and said bring us fish. Other faces at other tables were white with happiness. Heads went back to let out the throat gurgle and show the teeth. Our jewels were discreet. We all wear the bright eyeballs tonight. My eyes have green centers. After I got my legs loosened under the table and nicely folded one on the other I said after smelling, this fish is fine. Smells come to me now of a strange nature and one particular one which my sensibility thinking of your sensibility makes me not want to mention. But it is this foolish thread of adventure which is woven in me so when she said.

'My Charlie, you is big and nice.'

Eyes on her heart I dipped my face in the soup which I was eating with the fish and arranged the wind in my chest.

'Cynthia I am glad you have said that.'

'Charlie, it was you who made me love you. Ha ha, you have the amplitude of a warehouse.'

'Same to you.'

'But kidding aside. But Charlie, I want marriage more than anything.'

'It's the trouble I'm having.'

'But we could be having a baby. Charlie, don't you want to reproduce? Don't you want me to have your child?'

'Hold it, Cynthia, hold it. In the nature of this argument where it seems we are not avoiding the facts, let me tell you something.'

'I'm not a business acquaintance, Charlie. It hurts me when you talk like that. Why don't you be honest.'

'Marriage will destroy me.'

'Charlie I like you. Look at me. I'm a woman begging for a baby.'

'I'm telling you twice, marriage will destroy me.'

'But what do you do with your free time anyhow, Charlie, tell me that.'

'I roller skate. If my tailor didn't object to rough treatment of my garments I'd ice skate too.'

'See your pastimes are useless.'

'Cynthia, I had to work hard for what I am now. I was not exactly born in the gutter but I am now what I wasn't then and look what happened to my friends. You want to know what happened. No, you don't. Jake is surrounded. He is surrounded by humanity which is of his own making. Don't tell me it's a joke to have orange juice squirted up the nose by upstarts started with a jump in bed and maybe some ceremony that costs a lot of money. Don't tell me, why Jake is grey before his time. Why Jake sits there rubbing his hand over his head, speechless, stupid with the effort of fending off four savage kids. Sure Jake says standing in the lobby of my apartment, I'm sorry Charlie for the broken table. I said Jake, kids are no blessing I know but you don't have to pay me for the table. You think I want that.'

'We can plan parenthood.'

'What a laugh. Plan parenthood. You know what I'm like in bed. Maybe because you don't let me but how can I plan when I don't have the remotest control over my urges. When legally you got to give.'

'I could urge you not to.'

'Cynthia, God created us to do it. I'm not having any nonsense like that. Do what God wants you to, that's my motto.'

'Soon as I say something, you get like this.'

'Cynthia it's true. Why should I curb urge. Marriage is the sacred joining of two bodies where if God is willing two people can at last have a little fun. That's why I still keep in good shape. When use of my body is finally called upon I can throw it into action and in this throwing into action I don't deem suppression of my natural wildness as good for me. Besides my doctor says so. He said let your natural wildness go. Naturally I'm waiting for the ripe time. Boy you've been some help. My doctor says I'm all right.'

'Remember I've had medical overhauls too. Really complete and A one.'

'What, a specimen.'

'He examined me for three days.'

'Must've been fun. For myself my doctor only had to make me cough to see I was a specimen, a real one. Cynthia I'm svelte.'

'That's what you wish you were. You got your share of lard. And your doctor, ha ha.'

'He guided most of my family through their last illnesses.'

'Boy what a recommendation.'

'Cynthia, you want to know something. You really want me to tell you?'

'Let me tell you something, master-mind. Just let me tell you something. I don't need your body to get me pregnant. Just think of that one, will you, while you're at it. There are lots of men wandering around who would like what I could give.'

'What are you giving.'

'The companionship of an exciting mind. What I've wasted on you.'

'This is ruining the fish meal as well as the suitable libation.'

'We know you went to night school, Charlie.'

'Libation is a word I have been acquainted with since childhood. I'm too young to marry.'

'The way we argue about this marriage. For two years you kept saying it was money. Look at all the money you're making.'

'Don't forget my early struggle.'

'That's a real laugh. You started with one store. Then you got two. Then you got three. Then you sold them all. And got one big one. Then you got two. How could I forget your early struggle you repeat every time we go out plus all the things people did behind your back.'

'I'm proud to say Jake is still my friend. My struggle was real. My struggle was not an accident. Social acceptability is open to me everywhere but before that my friends deserted me and did most unkind things behind my back for which I have not forgiven them and for which I drove them out of business. Was I supposed to laugh when they put dynamite in a bathroom fixture, right in the house I live in, my home, tried to blow me up while I was shaving. You call that funny.'

'I call it funny you can't face a baby.'

'Why don't we eat the soup, the fish and libate. I'm tired tonight. I know you for too long, Cynthia.'

Cynthia with her high hair held with a spike of gold. Charlie, the love beast. I've always wanted to be a child of love. Like I am with things in my heart. In business they don't believe what the lips say, only what you get on paper. I'm not against babies. Or Jake's four kids. I love other people's little whippersnappers. I want Cynthia to come like a queen to my apartment. Right into my house. Maybe stopping outside the door to pick four lilies I grow there. I want her to hold them high. Rest them on her head. Then rest them on my head and take her hand to play in my hair. I want my door chimes to go on ringing. Those chimes are intimate to me. Because I chose them to play one single tune. A tune I heard after I closed my first big deal and was in a bus station where a kid was playing an instrument for a dime I gave him. I took that tune in my head back to my apartment. I sat down with a book and figured it out all by myself how to work it into chimes. Cynthia heard them and she told me if I ever wanted to marry her I better choke off those chimes. When she left after saying that, because I threw her out on her ass, I stuck a match in the bell. Went back to the living room floor and I cried. Only done that twice in my life. If that moment had only been otherwise, Cynthia, lilies on her head, put her hand in my hair which she wouldn't do unless I made her. Said maybe you have something I could catch. The chimes taught me a lot. In my own way, love is a thing I like to keep. Maybe it's a sound. A memory of a beautiful gesture. A keepsake of a king that I would be had four years ago she said sure Charlie I love you enough to let you do it. Her body has some fine lines. I don't want planned parenthood. To this day and from the day I met her through an introduction on the beach she teased me with the fine lines. These lines are not so swell now. I carried a cane with a fancy nob then and used it when I was only wearing a bathing suit. She thought it was so high class. I tried never to disillusion her from that observation. Four months later she was telling me a pair of striped trousers I was wearing was an obstacle to me going out with her. I put myself in the hands of the tailor, saves fighting, I say, blame him. I know what class can do to people and what people do to you if you don't have it. She said her father was an opera singer. Two months later I find it's a lie. I've been ashamed of my parents but I don't go around saying they sing operas. I tried to get her on the sand late at night on the beach the first day but the sandfleas were terrible. She said don't get too familiar.

'Hey Charlie, fussy face.'

'Me.'

'Charlie the fish, the soup, all charming. And the libation you have garnered the meal with is subtle. I'm glad you can live the way you do.'

'So am I.'

'But we're young no longer.'

'Cynthia, youth is not only being young. I have expanded with the years.'

'Charlie, I wish you had brutality.'

'What's this.'

'If you had been a real bull in the past.'

'Hold it Cynthia. Your suggestion is criminal.'

'I know.'

'Why did you make it for then.'

'It's exciting.'

'Don't try serving me with a dish of desire. I've had enough desire.'

'You were just thinking of me on the beach that night we first met, weren't you. I know the look.'

'I was not.'

'You were. You always think of it.'

'I regret you pressing me on this question.'

'Oh yeah.'

'I also regret you see fit to cast me in the shape of a person without candidness.'

'You were thinking of me on that beach with my brown legs. I was in the surf then, I was lovely.'

'Don't forget the sandfleas.'

'Don't forget how you said you desired me because you loved me.'

'Don't forget how you said I was the first man who ever said that to you so fast.'

'Charlie, how did our love stop.'

'Who said it stopped.'

'I'm not stupid Charlie. Our love stopped. I've asked you for mercy.'

'That's reasonable after four years of nothing.'

'I've asked you for marriage.'

'Yeah.'

'To take me as I am before it's too late.'

'Too late for whom, Cynthia, get it straight.'

'I want you to tell me you love me.'

'Eat your soup.'

'Like you did that Easter time.'

'The past is past.'

'I wouldn't care if it was only some remark like saying, Cynthia you doll, or something like that. Words don't matter so long as you mean them. Charlie, you chopped me down. You really cut me down. The happy time when I made you the strawberry cake. You ate it like a hungering animal and it was good to watch.'

'Naturally, that was all I was getting was the cake.'

'I was showing you my creative process in the home. That oven hasn't cooked a good thing since. Tell me why, Charlie. Why we sit here cut from each other. Sure you'll say when wasn't it like that. But even a libation doesn't lift the pall. I'm even glad you used that word tonight. I liked you for using it. I really did. I'm not changing my mind now just to please you. You've got command. I was thrilled by the way you ordered tonight.'

'Let's face facts, Cynthia. I asked them to mail the menu to me last week. I rehearsed what I was going to ask for tonight for three hours this afternoon till I was nearly hoarse. Just to ask for three items on a menu. This is no credit to me. I've got a whole heart, the pumping parts of which are not eternal, although to briefly make a play with words, it's internal. But don't fool me, Cynthia. Flattery only makes me uncomfortable after four years.'

'You still chop me down, Charlie. Chopping me right down.'

'Cynthia, you're not going to suck my blood in a marriage.'

'I swear I swear I won't do that.'

'Your bloom is gone. Now you want to give me a smell. I don't want to hurt your feelings. I'm not the large hearted person you take me for. I had a love for beauty. Still got one.'

'Charlie, you can take me tonight.'

'No.'

'Charlie, don't you want me.'

'No.'

'Charlie, please, a chance.'

'No.'

'It's over. You're telling me it's over.'

'It's over.'

'I didn't think it would happen like this. Charlie, can't we relive it. Just relive some of the nights we went out and had such fun.'

'Too expensive.'

'You think you had to buy me.'

'I bought you. I got companionship and comments on how I should behave to be able to keep paying you. Now tonight you make a special offer at half price.'

'I was only keeping it for later. Saving it. All girls have to save something. It would have been such a treat for you because you've wanted it for so long and I thought you would go for it and like it because you were starved.'

'What makes you think I was starved.'

'Aren't you starved for some.'

'I'm distinctly not starved for some. I even know a woman who likes it.'

'Oh.'

'No surfeit but I'm not starving.'

'Charlie, do me one favour. Don't look upon me in your memories as if I teased you with it.'

'That's not asking for much. I will look upon you in my memories as if I saw you for what you are. I've got to. I can't make this mistake twice.'

'You wouldn't even give me that. You wouldn't even let my memory be sacred.'

'No.'

'What would you do if I told you here and now I'm heartily sorry for what I did. That I'm heartily sorry. That I would do anything to undo what I've done, even though it took the rest of my life.'

'I'd tell you you were nuts.'

'Not one vestige of mercy left in you, is there.'

'No.'

'I guess I just finish eating and swallowing the libation. Just like that. Just like squeezing this lemon. Then throw it away.'

'Whose juice got squeezed out, not yours.'

'Is there any use asking for another chance. If on God's earth there is anything I can possibly do to bring us together, you'll tell me won't you.'

'No.'

A Grave

I was on my back with a book at midnight in Connecticut. A storm filling the Housatonic River and a fox barking at the lightning coming down into this mountain of trees. They said on the last page that they buried Herman Melville on a rainy day in Woodlawn Cemetery on the outskirts of New York.

Later in the month I got on the train and went to the city to visit. Through Danbury, Stamford and New Rochelle and along the Bronx River where years ago they could sail a battleship. Now it's dammed, small and smelly from sewers. Lovers come down here in the summertime. And kids swim in the parts that are deep and twins once dived off a ledge and got stuck in the mud and never came up again.

I went up the steps of the station, stood on the bridge watching the cars on the new highway. All that smoothness, comfort and curves. Roll you everywhere on the soft wheels. I went through the big iron gates and up into a cool stone mansion with typewriters and quiet pleasant people. A young woman took me to a chair and table and went through the files. She came back with a card and a map and drew a line along the winding avenues to an x which she said was on top of a hill.

I strolled by all the marble, granite and bronze doors, late blossoms and lovely trees. In there richer than I am alive. A man in a grey uniform saluted and smiled. I climbed a little hill up fern and ivy lined paths and stopped under a great elm tree. There were four stones, one with a scroll and feather pen. Through the trees I can see the mausoleums and the stained glass and doors for giants. And down there on the New York Central tracks the trains are roaring by to Boston. I came here to see if it were true and it is. And as everywhere the gravestones say the voice that is silent the hand that is still or even my Mabel I'll never forget you till we're together again. I went reading and wandering until I went out the gate again.

A few blocks away I stepped into a bar called Joe's. And sat up on a high stool and ordered a glass of beer during this dark afternoon. A smell of cheese, oil and tomato pies. Some lazy jazz out of the juke box. Behind the bar a man with his white sleeves neatly rolled up on tough hairy arms said I've seen you here before a few years ago maybe five or six, I remember your face. Yeah I remember you, I never forget a face. Got a memory for faces. He brought me a shot of whisky and another beer and said this is on me. When I left he said yeah I'll see you again.

I walked back to the station and waited for the train. Others were going by bound north for suppers in the country, swaying on the center tracks with lovely lighted windows, white napkins and fresh evening newspapers. Some were aluminium with red stripes. Once in a while a woman would look at me from a train to Chappaqua, Valhalla and Pawling.

When I got back and drove along by the dark empty fields with round shadows of cedars and down my own lonely lane through the pines and further to the little clearing in the woods I heard the Housatonic rumbling below and three deer standing in the headlights. I had spare ribs with onions and lemon juice and a bottle of beer. After that I wrote a letter to a man in Europe and said,

Will we all
Be watering
Lawns
Sometime later
In Connecticut.

Thamn

The parade had started. With an impersonator stepping out from behind maples in Main Street and letting go with a few impersonations. His name was George and he could do some fine bird calls. The birds responding and landing all over his shoulders. In summer he popped ripe cherries down their throats.

The townsfolk looked upon George as a joke. And made some sly remarks about the State Asylum. If the facts were faced, certainly George was not all there. The girls especially treated George as a joke and laughed at a good distance. George was a fixture in town.

Until that day. Of the parade. When most of the townsfolk were called upon to do their little bit on the stage. George could imitate Popeye. The barber, Joe, had him around the shop and called upon George for his imitation as a side show for his customers. George was sent to buy peanuts as a prize, and the customers laughed. Only Mr Thamn the undertaker felt guilty. And he changed his time for a haircut.

Cornfields were ripening around town. Blowing tassels of cornsilk and an evening dust of seed into the sky. The setting sun got so fat and red these days. And the ground was white and hard around the bottoms of the maples in Main Street. At Bing's Diner and Learner's Hash House, the cross country truck drivers come in for coffee, wiping the sweat from their brows. The town was running short of ice cream.

The parade today turned left and marched along Napier Avenue making for the Glade. Words going through some heads to a tune the band was playing. Words forbidden by the High School Principal. And which were thought first heard some few years after the birth of George. Gossip having it that he wrote it himself.

> There's gladness
> In the Glade
> Where momma and daddy
> Made me.
>
> There's madness
> In the Glade
> Where momma and daddy
> Made me.
>
> Where momma and daddy
> Made me
> In the Glade.

The swimming water in the creek was low and the steps to the red high diving board were roped off. Some said the rattlers were out and biting. The drums of the band would scare them away into the rocks. George wore a blue shirt and tan cloth trousers. And round his neck was a string holding a jew's harp. Which he could play to beat the band.

The town of Moment got its name because it was where the train stopped for that long before they built the road. One hundred and twenty years ago it was settled by Swedes. Rangy types who twanged and hip swivelled around the General Store and any sharp street corners. At the graduation exercises Mr Thamn, who had been called upon to speak, said they were all God fearing folk, sending forth a youth who sprung from the heartland of America. There were many eyes filled with tears that day, for if nothing else, Mr Thamn knew how to pluck the heart strings. And all sweetness helped, specially since it was only a year after the bank swindle when a pillar of the town lit out quick for

Brazil leaving a vague jungle address behind. He had been a prize winner at graduation.

Mr Thamn was fat at the neck, small footed, with small blue eyes and pale soft skin. He had an open toed walk and tread the town quietly. His life had once, some years ago, been briefly touched by scandal when a little girl ran home to her father screaming that a man was standing watching her. The father came back to the woods, holding his little girl's hand, and he met Mr Thamn who said 'Good evening,' and the father said 'Good evening,' and the little girl said 'That's the man,' and the father said 'Hush, child.'

Some said Mr Thamn was such a nice man because he came from Switzerland to America when he was eight years old. Others did not care where he came from and objected that the town undertaker made cheese as a hobby and sold it in Zeke's General Store. They said it had a stink.

George lived in a cellar and tinkered with radios. A dark little tomb down steps at the end of a long alley. Lots of people said he was broadcasting the messages they got Fridays, which put the wind up most folk and brought family listening to a standstill. The State Police closed in one night with riot guns and they caught George surrounded by his wires, and when they closed their hands around him he squealed with high pitched sounds, and the chief said 'Let the kid go,' and they went out to the squad car and never bothered George again. George, town simpleton, twanger of the jew's harp and inventor of the front roller skate wheel for the bicycle.

This day of the parade there was a first prize for the best float. Little girls dressed by their mommies to look like princesses and little boys to look like kings. Blue was a color, and pink, and America was written with more blue and red and ribbons of white. The Episcopal Minister came smiling out of his church and waved a little flag and said 'Bon voyage to the Glade,' and the veterans said 'Why doesn't that bastard talk English.'

These floats, all flowered, pulled along by mommies and daddies, and one by a big dog who stopped to lift a leg at a parked car, and the folk laughed and the little girl cried and ran to her mother. Ahead the drums were beating, horns blowing. Stars and Stripes hanging from windows. And now the booming went down Napier Avenue where it was cool under the archway of trees.

By three o'clock they had reached the Glade. The parade moving across the dry cinder path, kicking up dust, past the horseshoe and shuffleboard courts and making a grey way on the green grass of the baseball diamond. Then down through a meadow where a rock stuck up out of the grass, a sad mark where a boy, twelve, from a family of thirteen, broke open his skull and the grass where his head lay seemed red for weeks afterwards, a priest blessing him and taking him in his arms to the ambulance. And later that night to Mr Thamn.

The crows were cawing and flying away to their nests in the tops of the trees. The band disassembling under the oak where the kids made tree huts and George had invented the tree swing, a rope tied high in the oak on which they dove and were swept up into the sky at a hundred miles an hour. Families were spreading out their picnics on the rustic tables. The beer barrels were set up in the shade surrounded by the veterans of foreign wars who had led the parade wearing their medals. George was wearing the Iron Cross.

The ice cream was packed in hot ice. Kids throwing it into the water fountain to make it smoke. Women sat passing out the sandwiches and hot dogs. Trucks had brought the pop coolers, now clustered with small fry handing over their nickels. One young mother smoothed down her dress and said 'I don't want the likes of George looking and seeing while he plays that mouth harp.' Often this was what George did. In a cunning fashion, head bent, thumb strumming, lids lowered on eyeballs, he would peek out under the trees and dresses. Until this day. Of the parade.

138

Mr Thamn was wandering from group to group. He put his fat fingers out on various heads of hair. Some women didn't like the touch of his hand. Mr Thamn's wife had died and was buried by him seven years ago this August. With lots of folk from the town tramping up through the gravestones as Mr Thamm stood and heard his assistant read the service. His dry face looked up at the sky and down at his hands, and finally he licked his lips when it was time to go back for the funeral lunch. He was often seen these late afternoons, as the leaves were turning, standing over the grave, eyes on the words deeply chiselled in the stone.

Ida Thamn
1918–1941
From the Bridal to the
grave in three short years

And every month of August her resting place was covered with purple roses which came on the refrigerator train.

The peak of the picnic was round about five. The running events were over, the three legged race, egg and spoon race and other embarrassing events in which some elders took part being a bit stoned. Tiny tots played ring around the rosy we all fall down. The stage had been set up under the oak, a flowered curtain drawn across and the red floor boards waxed for dancing later in the evening when the Chinese lanterns would be strung out and the band would sit playing tunes.

During the parade Mr Thamn had stopped twice to tie his shoelaces, bending over, making his black serge bottom glisten in the sun as the other paraders passed around him. People remembering a year when Mr Thamn with several members of a happy go lucky club were revelling during a convention and marched through the town at midnight wearing diapers and blowing horns. But Mr Thamn was mostly a man who went about his lonely business perhaps sitting on the benches by the Monument in memory of lives lost in a battle with the Indians.

And near this place was the road which led to the dump. Made of ashes and cinder. Where the town was filling in the swamp. And where George, catching turtles, wandered through the tall cattails wearing pails on his feet in the watery ditches. And sometimes Mr Thamn passed and asked if he was going to make soup.

Today of the picnic and parade. The dump with rats and snakes was a mile away through the woods. George's turn came to do his impersonations. With lower lip up touching his nose he was Popeye. And then sent his crow calls loud and clear into the woods. There was giggling as the crows called back. Playing his jew's harp, George finished with a hoof and stomp and with a final leap in the air, brought his feet together and bent his head. Clapping was long and loud.

Mr Thamn walked on stage raising his hands for silence, his stubby fingers outstretched, to give his little speech. He said he was very happy today to announce the prize winners. As the names came, Mr Thamn looked up and out into the audience with his small smile. The little folk rose sheepishly, with glances back at mommie and daddy as they said, 'Go ahead, child.' And up the steps to the stage where they curtsied or bowed and took the emblem and the ribbon. Until it happened.

Mr Thamn had read the name like all the others, his head looking up, the little girl taking leave of her parents and mounting the stairs to the stage. Her hand outstretched to take the emblem and the other to shake with Mr Thamn. And suddenly she pointed up at his face and shouted, 'Daddy, this is the man who watched me on the dump road.' Mr Thamn stepped back, taking away this little hand that clutched his shirt.

Mr Thamn went back and back, falling over the stool. The little girl clenched hands shaking at her sides. Her father making for Mr Thamn who scrambled to his feet, his face atwitch. Elders crowded in front of the stage.

George stepped out and with an arm held the father back from Mr Thamn. He said Mr Thamn is a good man and if anyone tries to touch him, I'll fix them. George took Mr Thamn by the arm. Led him down the steps and away out under the trees. Which were turning light gold on their edges this late afternoon of the parade.

My Painful Jaw

I walked through where people and women with legs crossed and furs sat on soft sofas and a man with white gloves pointed me into an elevator with gleaming brass doors. When it was nearly full they closed and green lights were buzzing and binging and I said five please. The doors opened. Before me a grill, a cage, a man in there. I took off a watch and with my wallet and some change put them into an envelope, pinched it up with a machine and handed it through a hole to the man. I walked down the rows of dark green lockers in near silence and darkness. Turning up a row and pulling on a light, I opened a little green door and took off my clothes.

When I went down some back stairs in my athletic garments I bounced on my rubber soled boots. I went into a room and put a pair of leather gloves on my fists and beat a bag like mad. I skipped rope watching my calves in the mirror. I went over to a window and looked out across the street into living rooms and kitchens or just on the sills at plants.

You could smell the sweat coming from me. I could. And I sat down. Stretch out in these soft warm towels and rest my hairy legs. People come in. Where of course some fear to tread because of fists. Around the walls are pictures of fighters with muscles others with smiles but all standing ready to punch. Most said hi, sat down and whenever they looked at me said boy you're in good shape. I said o no not really, my midriff is fatty and all the while I'd slowly expand out my chest. Then a bouncy man came in throwing blows in all directions looked at me and said how about a few rounds. I tried to look away, I didn't know where to hide my fists. But the eyes would be on me looking for any fear so I said certainly.

We got in the ring. Bong, the gong. Out in centre ring I threw what was a feeler or to see if perhaps he might stand well away from me in anxiety but biff right on my nose and bang on my jaw this man started beating me around the place. I didn't want to turn and run outright because they might think I wasn't taking my beating like a man. So I hid under my gloves to try to give the impression that I was only playing. He knocked me right through the ropes and in spite of everything I made an effort to giggle with o it's nothing I like a good fight but a tooth dropping out of my mouth just produced a splutter. I think my adversary said sorry old man and something in me made me smile through the blood as if I were only resting that round.

He put it to me, have you had enough old man. I said I like a good workout, gets up a sweat. I almost mentioned blood too. I rested in my corner waiting for the bell. When it rang I came out with my customary feeler to size up his style for my special zip punch which I am reluctant to use. We circled around. I must admit I stayed my distance only of course because my zip punch can be fatal at close quarters. The fight had aroused interest in the room, people pushing to see. I had firmly made my decision to use the zip. I think he knew what was coming because he kept his guard high, the only nearly adequate defense against this punch. I waited for the corner of my eye to see a few more people gather, and then I moved in. I brought it from the hip, my right knee slightly flexed, weight well forward on the balls of my feet. The last thing I heard was the little audience catching a collective breath.

They told me later when I was dressed and showered that for awhile they didn't think I'd come around and someone even suggested giving me artificial respiration as well as the salts. But it was generally agreed that in final analysis it was better that this had happened because the zip punch, especially with the stance I was employing, would have been deadly. My opponent now wearing a bow tie clapped me on the back and said I was a hard man to hit and are you sure you're all right old man. I was horrified when my mouth said I'd very much like to have another workout with you sometime.

I Failed

I got off at the back gate out of a green upholstered tram. This first day. And there was the university through my apprehensive eyes. A chill wind blowing. My new suit, white shirt and black tie. I felt all dressed up for failure but feeling important because they were looking at me. There's the porter's lodge and a parking lot and in this building I see the contortions of glass, bubbling pots and skylights poking out of the roof. I want so much to learn. To know what you do with acids and esters and make my experiments go pop at the right time like the rest of you. From the very first word you tell me I'm going to remember.

I'm on my way to my tutor. Through these playing fields flat green and velvet. How lovely with benches where I can sit watching, reading or anything under those old trees. I think late summer is still hanging in the sky. And by these flower beds still smelling, into this pretty square where the opulent members of college live behind granite and big windows. That's me. I see a man filling a pail of water from a green pump. He salutes me with a wave. How can I make a good impression, tuck my tie in, smile perhaps. I hope they will see I'm eager, ardent to listen, ready to take notes for all four years.

That building there must be the library because I can see the stacks and stacks. I will borrow and read. I promise. What luck has brought me here because it's all so beautiful. I'm told scholars can play marbles on the dining hall steps and shoot birds in college park. Got some great rules. Perhaps some day will see me shooting with the best of them. There are little clusters of students and I can hear their beautiful voices as I go by. And I can't help but look from face to face seeking out those who will also fail. The rest of my natural life without a degree. I almost wish now some little white angels would flutter down and take me or my dread away.

Across the cobbled square a bell ringing and into this building number eight. Up the foot carved stairs where I see an open door. I'll knock lightly so's not to be rude. Hands out of pockets. Do the right thing. Always wait till asked. Come in. From behind that door he's telling me to come in. How shall I do it without making noise with my heels. I said as best I could that I was D and he said ah delighted, do come in. Piles of papers everywhere and books. Must have been here like this since God. Great waves of hair on this man's handsome head, a scholar in Greek and Latin for sure. Ah D I'm very glad you're here and I trust your trip across the Atlantic was pleasant. My God, this gentleman is telling me he is glad I'm here and what can I say. I can say nothing, there's no chat in me because I'm trembling. I hope it won't mean some awful thing's to happen. He's only being nice and saying, now D I would like you to meet Hartington, it is Hartington isn't it. And this tall tall person standing in a shadow stepped out, said yes and offered me his hand. You're to share rooms together. I tried to say splendid, couldn't, and said safely how do you do. Our tutor rustled in the papers, came out with pamphlets and said I hope you will be very happy with us here Mr D. And now what could I say, trapped on this casual note of friendship. I did so want them to know that I knew I would be, but it was too late, no space left to tell them I was overjoyed to silence.

On that cold morning in October I came away from that old room filled with books and papers with this strange tall person walking beside me who asked softly and slowly won't you come and have coffee. I was scarcely able to say thank you I'd like to, but I was smiling so pleasantly willing to please.

You Murdered My Cat

I put all my little trunks and things strewn in the hall. A gobble of little rooms where I came cheaply to live in peace. I grew flowers of a geranium kind in my window box. And hung streamers all colored to flutter away the birds. My Sunday stew was a cloud of wonderful smells. Let them out one by one. A cosy comfort in the sky. Because I thought these neighbours would love me more.

And in the April of the year I bought a cat. Little bumbling tender ball of life. I paid a pound and called him Scratchy. And months went by till he knew me by my smile. And tender steak I sacrificed for his own red joy. He got big, wide and strong. Some cat. And met me every six, all seasons, at the door. A nice little whine all for me. Two globes in his head that glowed my own happiness.

Scratchy was a wilful cat. I wasn't blinded by that soft, blue fur and cocked sad head looking at my own. Scratchy had his mischief, as what cat hasn't. Running with tail straight up and straight up the furniture. I didn't mind the few scars streaked on the odd antique. After all, who would want an old sourpuss cat. He had his faults, and as I say, what cat hasn't.

And I never knew he was musical. Until once his ears sat up as I piped out a little tune on my recorder. Even sold my plastic one for real wood. I could tell he appreciated the change. He liked the melodies of the Old South. My specialty. And I know no one will believe it, because he would do it only for me, but Scratchy could get up on his hind legs and dance like a real cat. Only thing ever frightened him was the big pipe I made the foghorn noise with. Some cruel thing came out in me every now and then and made me want to make him cringe, back up with a real tiger snarl, and spit right 'cross the room. Almost felt I was in the jungle fighting it out for my life. He knew I was only kidding. And we respected each other for what we were. I was doing accountancy at the time.

But that Easter, when all the trees were greening and Scratchy raced in shrubbery as I tried to lead him through the park, was his last. You somehow know the cat hater. They have a look they wear right across the eyes. Spill water on a defenceless animal's head and say it's an accident. And they lived the other side of the garden. Hear them grinding in and out at all hours in fast cars. Type put their own mothers in institutions. Blaring radio and all the rest. I was never deceived in the beginning by that sweet smile and how's little Scratchy today. They hated Scratchy. Said he dug up the gladioli and pretty stunted efforts they were, anyway. And they said he did other things as well. Look what he's done. I said look here. They said look there. I know my own cat and he would never do a thing like that. I raised him from a kitten. And then there were threats.

You just touch Scratchy and I'll report it to the police. No one's touching your dear little Scratchy, wretched revolting thing. I could have killed them publicly right then and there and be pleased to hang for it.

I kept Scratchy in after that. Rather than expose him to their malingering hands. I'm not one for drawing definite distinctions, but I think if a person doesn't like animals there's something wrong. Dumb things who depend upon our indulgence and love. Let me watch someone's behaviour for five minutes with a dumb animal and I'll tell you what he's like.

I had got Scratchy his new basket for Christmas and made it all soft and warm with a Manx rug. He went to it each night and I left the garden window open just to give him that little freedom. And that night I was fast asleep. I dreamt I was driving a motor scooter in Lapland. Across barren wastes with no end in sight. And that a great black bear behind a mountain, and bigger, peeked out and growled and the whole world shook. I was awake in an instant. I heard the door slam across the yard. A slaughter sound. I ran to Scratchy's bed. It was still warm and he was gone. I whistled from the window. But a cold hand touched my heart. I saw their basement light go off.

And in the morning I went out and stood there in the sunshine. A back garden in despair. If any of them were looking out of the windows they knew what I was thinking. I went straight to the police.

Meet My Maker

I set out one summer singing. To meet my Maker. He lived on a hill with lawns around and buttercups sprinkled in the green. I said I'll climb your hill and knock on your door, look in your windows and see what I saw. He came out in a pair of blue jeans with a pipe and said hi, when did you die.

I told him yesterday about noon. They all stood around for my doom. Even Sidney in his sun glasses and Flora just out of her red sports car. They looked at me and said he's gone for a ride and that's all I heard when I died.

And Maker said come in and sit down. He said sherry. I said pale please and dry. Now tell me young man how was your trip, were some of the stops called despair and did you see the town called sad. Or did you detour through laugh. Maker I'll tell you the truth I stayed too long in the metropolis called money which I found to be sunny, a city of aspic, tinkle and titters where I bought at the bottom and sold at the top.

But son surely you didn't stay. Maker I did and never left till my dying day. I lived way up in the sky with a terrace where I sang my song:

> Every tulip
> Is a julep
> And all the mint
> Is meant for me.

And Sidney and Flora came and said why don't we have some fun and go up to Vermont for a barbecue. And all night we drove through the beer cans along the road. I sat looking out between the trees and at others racing along and I thought I'm weak and want to belong. To clubs and leisure life and breathe only imported air. But Flora said I was the sensitive type who looked well with a pipe and could afford to be poor if I wanted or even maybe something real special so that they'd all be glad to know me later on. But I said no I want to be loved for my money and nothing else will do. So off we went to Vermont for the barbecue.

Out by the lake we lit a fire, spread out the marshmallow and steak. And Maker this is why I never had a chance to repent. I just thought I'd go for a swim and look up at the stars and then sat around and got a chill and later I knew I was ill. So I said before I was dead take me back to the city of money fast and see how much they charge to get out of this. And they came and said buddy you're on your way to the next town and this here train can't turn round. So I said where's the ticket taker maybe he personally knows my Maker because I have a few things he can buy at the bottom. But they said there is no ticket taker because this ride's free.

So Maker I just said gee and as you can see I never had courage to give up the salmon and riesling or the picnics at Newport but stayed at my club for showers and grub and could never get enough. Son, cheer up, I know how you feel, but let me tell you we have some fine vintages here as well as delectable veal. And oceans of time and beef in its prime. So relax and watch the sun shine. But Maker how can you welcome me from that land down there when I've never been kind or felt any despair. Son, I can see you never meant any harm, another helping of the peaches and cream is no need for alarm.

But Maker, what about Sidney and Flora. Son, come over, you can see them from here. Wow, Maker, can you see all this. Son, behind every and any blind. But Sidney's got my cigarette lighter and Flora my flat, why those cheapskates, I'll never forgive them for that. Easy son, that's what you were like before you got up here. But Sidney's playing my gramophone and Flora's taken my Ming horse. Son, next time leave nothing behind and you'll feel no remorse.

Well, Maker, what do we do now. Son, it's time for a swim and workout in the gym and after a good scrub I'll take you to a nightclub. But Maker I can't see how we so readily agree, this is even better than it was down there and it's free. Son, look me in the eye and see what you see. Whoa, Maker, you're me.

Gustav G

The purple house with the peeling paint was in Gardenia Road in a western district of London. Five minutes walk beyond the social pale. It stood some yards back from the road with a front garden neither neat nor mussed. The windows gleamed. And inside all smelled of lavender wax and the floor boards creaked.

It was October, the month before the fogs which clung to this flat area and the year before had killed prize cattle at an exhibition up the road. After his wife left him, Gustav had come here to live with another woman called Queenie and brought his two dark haired daughters. Across the road was a club for Australians who reveled late at night singing songs of Down Under and emerging in the wee hours to crank their vintage cars.

Gustav G was tall, light brown haired, and an ex Polish Cavalry officer. With drink taken, his manner often insisted upon his impeccability. Which his English wife had found painful. At these times, Gustav rummaged in the wardrobe, fetching out from the moth balls his riding breeches and boots to stomp indignantly into the onion reek of the kitchen adjusting his insignia and rapping his crop against his thigh.

'I am a true Pole.'

His English wife, pressing back her hanging hair, turned toward the onions and sliced on. Gustav retreated to the bedroom where he stood in front of the full length mirror, eyes swelling with tears. And later his wife packed up and left.

Gustav met Queenie during three bereft alcoholic days

and wove her into his life and she found them the flat of
three rooms in the purple house. With one narrow bed for
his two daughters. And mornings as the traffic increased
on the road outside, Gustav pulled back the covers in the
front room and reached for cotton wool and Eau de Vie
de Lavande with which he wiped cheeks and brow and
cleaned his awaking nostrils. Behind the house was a rail-
way siding and coal yard and the black dust seeped up
between the floor boards under the carpets.

Queenie went out to work each morning as a secretary
in a factory making nurses' uniforms. Taking a tortuous
trip through the fashionable parts of London to disappear
at the other end beyond a bleak door in a bleak wall of
Camden Town. Often she brought home lengths of white
cloth for dusters. Gustav with some clever folding sported
these as hankies in the breast pocket of his blazer. When
many a lonely afternoon between whiles, he stood stiffly
and sadly clutching a pint of beer in the basement shadows
of an airless drinking club.

Weekdays while he waited for a great pot of porridge
oats to cook, Gustav plunged his two daughters into the
tub for a wash. Sometimes retreating from the wild splash-
ing to pop on a threadbare silk shirt, the fortunate colour of
his skin. And with gay cravat, black sword stick, grey
flannel trousers and sports coat, he cut a figure and struck
several early morning poses in the doorway. Later standing
in one final attitude as his daughters wolfed through the
porridge.

At ten to nine he led them down the stairs and at the bottom in a blood tinted light, he made some comments he
knew would seep under the landlady's door.

'Amanda and Laurinda, you must pay strict instructions
to your riding master, straight back, remember.'

These daughters with their long dark tresses, standing,
waiting for Gustav to open the door.

'O daddy, please shut up.'

Gustav stomping sword stick, the stick leaving the sword as he stood in the hallway, waving the glistening blade.

'Do not speak in that fashion. One day you will listen. When I die, you will listen.'

'Daddy we know you'll die, but we're late, will you please give over.'

And the taxi passing in the road was flagged down with Gustav's stick. A clipped command to the driver as he held the door open.

'The Lycée, please, haste.'

Gustav leaning back in the leather comfort. Amanda sitting facing this father.

'Daddy Queenie is going to be furious.'

'I will not have you riding on buses.'

'You're wasting the money Queenie slaves for, you know we can't afford a taxi.'

In silence they reached that alley with the smooth accents, mothers, chauffeurs, intellectuals. Gustav led Amanda and Laurinda. He held his chin high and blinked his lids. He sniffed frequently with his nose. And flicked a finger in the corner of his eye. He stood by the doorway of the yard as Amanda took Laurinda by the hand and they fled across the bright concrete into school.

With an audible click of heel, Gustav turned and marched out the alley into the thriving life of South Kensington. He looked in the window of the harp shop and hummed a Hungarian Rhapsody. He waited loftily to cross on the black and white safety stripes, a girl in a gay white sports car stopping and he gave her a little bow and she grimaced and nearly killed him as she roared past. Gustav took her license on yesterday's bus ticket, the pencil constantly going through the cheap paper until it was a series of holes and he threw it away.

In his pocket he jingled six and sixpence, gritting his teeth at the expense of the taxi ride. Measuring in his mind his second breakfast in the Continental coffee house just past the station. Where collected the former members of deposed European governments and there was a warmth of food and greetings. Gustav took a seat at the window and reaching out touched the leaves of a prospering aspidistra. Marianna, the waitress, smiled and said, 'Good morning sir.'

'Good morning Marianna. I would like coffee with fresh cream and apple strudel. And how are you today Marianna.'

'Not good. And you.'

'Not good.'

Out the window frosty air and curled brown leaves scraping across the shadows of trees. The young students passing on their way to learn of art and some science at the colleges up the road. The girls wore hair long and careless. Gustav saw Amanda and Laurinda growing into these assured nubile young women floating by. But, my God, where was the money to come from and even a dignified place to live. There might never be a good address again. But the apple strudel was fine today. Just as it was fine yesterday and the day before. The juice had a light sweetness and the pastry melted in the mouth. There were young apples in Poland. And woods and forests around Malkinia some miles from the river Bug in the province of Warsaw.

His English wife had not been unpleasant. She never questioned his background or military rank or honours. She would, as she sliced through the onion, sigh, and say yes, how nice, I heard you, that was nice, I'm glad you loved the peasants on your estates and cried and danced with them. And how one day, the last day, he found his hands reaching for the pots, the pans and how they seemed to go through the windows, glass showering down, a great mirage of curtains, sash cord, and putty. Later feeling hands leading him by the arms. Blue uniforms ushering him to a seat in the back of a dark van. And a woman with gaudy mouth smiling at him. 'What did they get you for, dearie.' They brought water to the cell whenever he requested and led him slowly out for natural acts whenever he asked. And further in the dismal morning of that last day they let him free with a yellow slip of paper to make his way to the dock where the judge said it's sad to see a man of your background behaving in this fashion, pay ten pounds.

The incident received a column in the Times, and with a careful fourpence Gustav bought this paper. Sitting, rustling it high in front of his face and clearing his throat, a pearl pin stuck in the silk around his neck and he had lain for three recuperative days between white sheets and brown blankets, a bowl of water, spiced with lemon juice and vinegar, on his bedside chair. He dipped a towel and laid it across his brow and eyes.

And now in this month of October there were western moist winds, the first smells of smoke at evening. With a place to live there was a quiet respectability in his life. And although it was lonely London, it was a city of freedom to hang or gas yourself if you so wished but please leave a note for the milkman to stop the milk and the news agents to stop the papers. I am Gustav G a foreigner. And if I let taxis run over me till Christmas in the middle of the road, they would pass by tapping their umbrellas, poor chap, he's trying to do himself in.

Queenie left instructions pinned outside the food cupboard. Sweep. Wipe. Wash. He felt she watched him as he took helpings of what he fancied. In his marriage he always got the biggest chop. Women who say they love you covet the choicest morsels for themselves. Then try to make you a mat. Trampling your dignity with the household chores. Who tell you to look at the employment board of the meat pie factory. And then call you a sneaky devil because you sit and enjoy an hour's sunshine in the Asian garden of the Victoria and Albert Museum. Where the fountain plays mid the lead sphinxes and the dark green leaves of the cherry trees stir.

Weeks quietly by in the purple house. Gustav repressing

his thirst for avocados for the sake of financial peace. There was the odd opera and Sunday evening concert at the Festival Hall where they held hands and squeezed during the passionate passages, later to walk out on the deck strung with stanchions over the river and watch the squat tankers plow dark ways on the ebbing tide. Later to stroll a long way home by the fairy lights of Battersea and the water's deep sweet smell.

Queenie had ridden to the hounds in the west of Ireland. And talked as Gustav talked about his cavalry days. She said some blustering pinched type once sounded the horn and upon the last soulful note promptly pitched face first in some cow softened mud. Gustav to his feet, slightly in his cups, declaring Queenie an equestrian gossip and the Irish, peasant pigs. Queenie, breasts heaving, hands straight down at her sides, eyes blazing, letting go with convent bred epithets. And next day Gustav found his riding boots gone. To discover them one week later in the window of a gentlemen's clothier near the Portobello market. Paper begonias in a Japanese vase, the glistening toes of his boots facing a water colour picture of the harbor at Lyme Regis.

To inquire after one's wardrobe in another's possession took courage. Gustav walked up the street reasoning with his dignity, pushing through the throngs of people surrounding the stalls. Returning with stiff carriage he entered the shop.

'I say.'

'What can I do for you, guv.'

'I say there, the window.'

'Yes guv, the window.'

'Those happen to be my riding boots.'

'It's all right guv.'

'It's not all right.'

'Now look guv, I paid good money for them boots.'

'All right, how much money do you want.'

'Well guv, as I say I paid good money, three pounds fifteen shillings they're going for.'

'Very well.'

Gustav spinning on his heel which was rapidly going down. Flagging a taxi. Arriving back at the purple house. Bounding up the stairs. Tearing the day's list of assignments off the wall and throwing it in the garbage. To the gas meter. One fork on one little lock. Just a bit of leverage. Gustav swept the shillings out into his pockets.

Back at the gentlemen's second hand clothier's. Gustav strode in, eyebrows aloft. Ladling the handfuls of shillings out on the counter.

'I say, guv, you been at the gas meter.'

'I beg your pardon.'

'Sorry guv, just a joke like. Some come in here you know, blokes rifled the gas meter. Wouldn't say a thing like that if I thought you'd really cleaned out the meter, wouldn't be manners.'

'If you don't mind, my boots, please.'

'Sure guv. I'll fetch them out of the window. Good quality boot.'

'I think you'll find sufficient shillings there.'

'Sorry guv about the crack about the gas meter. It's like we're all human. Some folks these days take a penny from an orphan. It makes you think.'

'Good day.'

'So long guv.'

Gustav entered a public house where they drew wines and spirits from the wood. In the mahogany interior he put back mugs of claret reading a little sign against the decanter stand.

> Claret is a close friend
> To take wherever you go.

These were solemn times. Good blood flowed through his veins and even in the veins of some close relatives. On winter nights he had come out to the hovels on the plains and given gifts to their peasants, sacks of potatoes and turnips. They were ungrateful. And snarled behind your back. But the air at night had the distant bark of dogs and the chimney smoke and fires glowing at tiny windows when you pounded by. Horses loved the moonlight.

On this Friday, shilling Friday, in this snug public house, Gustav recalled other Fridays. With one hand in the pocket to take out more shillings for more claret. A taste of musky death. Like the rafters of the purple house. Three weeks ago there was the funeral of the Russian bishop. Laying the prelate to rest on this flat land of white stonery and overgrown paths between forgotten graves spreading everywhere. Chanting through the streets. He had dressed in full uniform. Stepping into the road, patting the coal dust out of his cuffs. Taking his place in the long line of mourners in their raiment. Executing the slow march when necessary. Taking a sprinkle of balm upon his person.

And this early evening, boots in brown paper bag. At this bar. Hiding in the north of London. When one ought to be meeting one's daughters from school. But claret calls, and you hear singing. On Moscow Road near here is the Russian Church. The mornings when one walked cold and cheerless, coatless, dragging two reluctant kids. Tune the ears to listen to the song chanted, the kids kicking your shins saying, 'When is it going to be over daddy.' And as Gustav waited for the bus, lost in memories happier, his youngest daughter gently leaned over and sunk her teeth in his thigh. Gustav reared up screaming in agony, the local windows opening. The bus queue laughed.

And tonight winter is coming down the road, the gas fires are lit everywhere. To the barman wrapped in white.

'I should like another bottle of Latour.'

'Certainly sir. The half.'

'The whole.'

'Very good sir.'

'And a sliver of Cheshire.'

There were other Friday memories and indignities. Connected with gentlemen's second hand clothier's. Friend of Queenie's, a particular revolutionary from Ireland. Who was to blow up Waterloo Bridge when the signal to take over England was given. And the night they asked him to baby sit and returning they found their pound of chopped steak gone and reposing in its place was a kipper. Later, a sheepish apology over many drinks was that the Irishman, who was overcome with an awful thirst for meat and not having been able to control himself, devoured it. For he had work to do for the cause, and he hoped they understood and enjoyed the kipper which ounce for ounce had more nourishment. However, he did not relish fish himself.

A chill outside tonight, along these hard bitten streets. In the lonely steamy windows women boiled cabbage and others smoked the air with sausages under the grill. Gustav's boots stood in their brown wrapping at his feet. He was at attention as he swirled, sniffed, and tasted the wine. Queenie was a good skin. She was young and headstrong. Who took him and his children to her large bosoms. And on those nice nights when she placed the glass of honeyed milk on the chair and unfolded the convertible sofa, gently so as not to smother in the dust, there was peace. A candle burning to kill the brownness general in all directions. Two little daughters asleep in the next room as they lay a head at each end of the bed, clutching each other's feet, chubby cheeks soft on the pillows.

Pay night across London. Friday faces, lit up eyes, heavy wrists with heavy hands, the grey overcoats crowd in. Gustav remarking between the heads.

'I should like another bottle of Latour.'

'A little more cheese, sir.'

'I think the cheese, too.'

Lights go on. Hold out the night and winter. He had been

taking bus routes which skirted all the agonizing parts of town. Until he now ended up on the water bus from the Zoo to Paddington. The Irishman had said he often used this boat trip to confuse Scotland Yard. Which recalled the next time they had this Gael baby sit which was the last time. When they returned to find him gone and a note.

Dear Gustav,

I cannot disclose any more information. But the uniform and boots will be returned after the present operation in the best of condition.

P.S. I was also forced to take the street map of Warsaw. All the best.

Ryan

And tonight as the white grey fog drifts down on the street and shifts in under the doors of this mahogany public house, Gustav G cried out suddenly.

'It cannot last.'

As the people turned to stare and some to edge away, Gustav looked deeply into the dried blood color of his wine. Open the escape valve when the boiler is throbbing with pressure. Queenie often resorted to this practice in public places, rearing up and often as she shouted, fleeing the premises. She said it prevented violence. And the first time she had ever done it was the most embarrassing he had ever known. It happened one Thursday before Friday payday and in the purple house he had gone to the water closet for a natural act in the dark. For the light switch was bust. And as he groped for paper, he felt only clammy wall on all sides. There was nothing for it but to get some scrip from one's pocket. He had reached in and found a tiny piece, most appropriate he thought as it was a canceled Sweepstake ticket. He used this paper and then set forth to the local public house where he was to meet Queenie and some friends.

Queenie had entrusted to him their last ten shilling note that morning to buy bread. And she waited with these persons one of whom had a goatee. Gustav entered. Stomping and hoofing in a rather reserved but definite way. He joined the joyful group and asked what would they have. Pints were ordered. Gustav digging in his pocket for the ten shilling note. Deeper and deeper digging in the pockets. And he felt the piece of paper and drew it out. Looking at it, a sudden wave of blankness came over him. He read the conditions of the Sweepstake ticket over and over. Queenie asked him what was the matter, to pay for the drinks. And Gustav set again to searching for the note. All pockets now hanging out. Whipping off his jacket, tugging at all trouser flaps. Making a great act of looking in his cuffs. Queenie asking how a ten shilling note could have got there. And suddenly as the search for the ten shilling note was finished, Gustav's past life passed in front of his eyes. Then he laughed. And assuming a dignified stance he recounted to them the story of the ten shilling note and how it must now be heading in some lonely sewer deep under the city toward the river Thames in the neighbourhood of Fulham.

It was then that Queenie shouted. And rushed out into the night. Gustav overcome. There were times when one could only collapse in tumult and clamor and laugh. Which did not last long. For returning, Queenie lay in wait. Gustav entering well oiled. She sprang from behind the door driving him through the flimsy coat cupboard wall. He felt his boots sticking into his back. Queenie was like a lioness. As she was on top savaging him, he was curious that the only thought that went through his mind was that he had not uttered a sound but went down and suffered in silence. Military training never left one. The fingernail treatment of the face was another matter. He finally got hold of her wrists and held them off. As she raged. Shouting, our last ten shilling note, you bestial Pole.

And even that altercation passed. It was good tonight to remember things. Certain incidents, if enough time had elapsed, looked colorful in one's background. He did not like the landlady. Or people who lurked behind doors for long periods of time. Women marry weak men but take strong lovers. He was perhaps a nice combination of the two. At least his wife had left him completely. Never hearing of her much except his daughters' fortnight visit to her somewhere in the northeast of London.

This Friday night was a night upon which one might draw conclusions. And avoid convulsions. Taking hold, perhaps, of a few minutes of the past. Thereby looking into the future. And now no horse, without which the bed-chamber was the only proper place for a gentleman to take exercise. And there in love, to guide one's little ship on the wide wide sea. Hoping for the winter ahead to be mild. And the frost was collecting on the stone statues in Gardenia Road as they stood ghostly in the garden at night. The black smoke stack of the meat pie factory. Crabitch, the pawn broker around the corner who ended up custodian of his boots and uniform when they vanished with the Gael. The church of the Methodist Connection, into which he had almost been persuaded. The funeral furnishers. There were those too. And when that day came. His turn with appropriate military honors. His coffin with insignia, medals lying on it and the white silk. Perhaps his rank was not sufficient for a march through the streets, however, there would at least be an occasion. Queenie would weep. His wife would go her cowlike way at the back, saying, I knew the bastard for what he was. The Gael had promised to bring up the rear with an Irish ass.

Tonight in this mahogany pub over the claret. Folk were keeping their distance. They wondered what they could see in the paper parcel. But they wouldn't find out. Tonight was the night of drinking, recalling yester months and days. A memorial service to himself. How sad and wistful one was. To push aside light brown and grey hair. To pass the high tide of years and begin the ebb. Queenie was twenty-seven summers. And sometimes she woke late at night and said what's that coming in the window. It was these times as he laid a sympathetic hand on her bare back that he liked Queenie deeply. Women, often the hard ones in daylight, woke fearful as dreams closed in. And horsemen hammered around the laneways. Her tattered underwear was sorrowful. His whole hand fitting through a great tear. Take her head on his shoulder and press back her hair. And she's asleep and never knew how good he was to her in the dark. Only for her to rear up in the reality of the next day and let fly with epithets.

Now there were more men parking their bicycles outside. And inside just this lucid liquid. Emitting the shout had left him much elbow room. And there would be no joining in other's conversations for most of them would be about him. And he could only think of a strange songless tune.

> No limelight
> Wherever
> This wretched Pole
> Lamented.

The English language was nice. He was glad of his alacrity with it. Broken as it sometimes was. On the other hand his accent was one of quality. He had behaved himself in this foreign country, albeit one or two little altercations. For which he now substituted the public shout. Working class men were drifting in. Stiffly making their way to the bar with their comments and money ready. He was not like other Poles who growl as people come close or sit next to them. These new arrivals had not heard him shout. It was like time itself, nothing lasts. And they looked upon him as just another bloke. All extending their pleasures in this pub.

To return tonight, O my God, to the purple house in

that evil road. A sunflower grew in another front garden near. And when that died he would die. That was the symbol. The little gas meter's door would be hanging open. And Queenie would come in. It was her epithets he could not stand. It was frightening. And as a father he shouted his two little kiddies into tears. Two defenseless creatures who wanted only that their daddy be nice to them.

Queenie would be out looking the streets and pubs for him. Track him down for the sneaky act of emptying the meter. This was no way to enjoy claret. To lurk now in absolute fear of her rage. He must go back. Back to the purple house in that evil road. With those curtain tugging, evil whispering upper working class people. With his own class nothing but a relic.

Gustav took up his parcel of boots. He walked out the door, a silent austere figure, and stood for a moment in the murky air. A distant prospect of a long line of lights disappearing down the road. He undid his laces and leaning up against the iron fence pulled off his shoes and slipped his feet into the boots. He stomped and walked forward. Shoulders back. Head erect, he marched up Kensington Park Road. Between the tall grey Victorian houses. His heels clicking on the side walk. One shoe under each arm. Ahead the lights of Notting Hill Gate.

Gustav G marched on jobless and drunk. And last night he had a dream. He dreamed he came around a street corner like the one ahead. And in front of him stood a figure he recognized. His wife. And when he said come and have a drink she fixed him with a stony eye. She side stepped to pass. He shouted, 'Didn't you hear the story of the ten shillings. What about that.' And his wife was running. And although Gustav was no slouch in dreams he could not catch her. And he had to stop against a wall to find his breath and a figure came out on an iron trellis balcony and said down to him as he lay against the bricks, 'God love all little children.'

Climbing on a bus, Gustav sat by himself up front. And got off at Gardenia Road. He walked toward the purple house in the fog. A lone light glowed up in the cold window, misted with steam. Gustav rang the bell. Waiting in the chill. Footsteps on the stairway. Coming down. He would have to dodge the first few blows. The door opening, he ducked and lifted an arm. Standing watching him was his wife. He said, 'O my God.' She said, 'Come in, you better go up the stairs.'

Gustav reading a strange message on her face. Climbing the stairs he paused outside in the hall. Through the crack of the door he saw his two daughters clutching themselves in the back bedroom. Queenie lay with her head in her arms at the dining table, the burning light bulb over her head. And he was near the fireplace and the oatmeal box on the mantel, watching. His wife came in. A sober strange little scene considering he had emptied the gas meter only that afternoon.

He stood accused. In all this silence. With the brown curtains hanging so limp and long at the windows. The air around the drafty panes billowing them out as buses roared by on the road. Both women in his life were present. Surrounded by security. Women protected you. Held the world at bay. You could push them ahead to buy tickets, groceries, even to a little innocent stealing at times. Traces of youth should still be with me. Especially needed now in a setting like this. One wife, one mistress. Two kinder. One purple house. Several aluminium pots and pans. Many cracked plates. Lots of useless lace at the edges of things. Women who antagonize the same man have something in common. Certainly he had not associated with women beneath him, nor very far above.

There were some quiet sobs. Queenie looked beaten. Did they both see the open gas meter. Then called a general consultation to put him down. In the next room the children were quietly crying. Two little girls holding each other.

Gustav looking from one face to another, sheepish in his boots. Finally putting his shoes on the floor. Putting a hand up to his cheek and rubbing it once. Had the gas company trapped them and caught them with the meter busted. Gustav spoke. 'What's the matter.'

His wife turning and looking out toward the window. Queenie unmoving, head in arms. Sobs from the kids. Gustav going into the children's bedroom. They were draped over one another on the bed. Laurinda, tears in large brown eyes.

'Daddy, I am getting smaller and smaller and when I've got small enough, I won't be alive any more.'

'Do not cry over that. You're growing big.'

'Mommy is taking us away, daddy.'

A taxi came at eleven late at night. Amanda and Laurinda went down the stairs with a little bag each. Queenie and Gustav stood at the doorway and waved as the car pulled away and went past the white frosty statues of the garden across the street. The next morning the note was already under the door from the landlady. This is a respectable house and be out of the premises by Friday. Gustav picking it up. Reading the message written in an evil hand on the lined paper.

On Friday morning, Gustav rose from his bed. Wrapped in his yellow dotted robe, he padded across the floor boards and dusty brown carpet. There were some blue thistle flowers in a vase. He picked one and held it in his hand as he moved into the hallway and down the flight of stairs to the water closet. This was the coldest closet in the world and gave out upon the blackness of the coal yard. He stood there over this white morning bowl. A quick glance at the busted light switch. Opening both eyes. Pushing the window up and looking to the horizon of distant tracks and the arches of a bridge. A church steeple. A red underground train curving on the tracks. If the landlady popped up the stairs to see if they were gone, he would offer her this thistle.

Antagonize her mind somewhat. People took no notice of other things if you carried a flower. As a child, his tutor, a distant impecunious uncle, had taught him this. Carry a flower through life Gustav and even if there is tragedy there will be fragrance and beauty as well.

More about Penguins

If you have enjoyed reading this book you may wish
to know that *Penguin Book News* appears every month.
It is an attractively illustrated magazine containing
a complete list of books published by Penguins and
still in print, together with details of the month's
new books. A specimen copy will be sent free on
request.

Penguin Book News is obtainable from most
bookshops; but you may prefer to become a regular
subscriber at 3s. for twelve issues. Just write to Dept
EP, Penguin Books Ltd, Harmondsworth, Middlesex,
enclosing a cheque or postal order, and you will be
put on the mailing list.

Note: *Penguin Book News* is not available in the
U.S.A., Canada or Australia

The Ginger Man

J. P. Donleavy

In the person of *The Ginger Man*, Sebastian Dangerfield, Donleavy created one of the most outrageous scoundrels in contemporary fiction, a whoring, boozing young wastrel who sponges off his friends and beats his wife and girl friends. Donleavy then turns the moral universe on its head by making the reader love Dangerfield for his killer instinct, flamboyant charm, wit, flashing generosity – and above all for his wild, fierce, two-handed grab for every precious second of life – *Time Magazine*

No one who encounters him will forget Sebastian Dangerfield – *New York Herald Tribune*

First published in Paris in 1955. An expurgated edition appeared in England in 1956 and in the United States in 1958. The complete and unexpurgated edition was brought out in England in 1963 and in the United States in 1965.

The Saddest Summer of Samuel S

J. P. Donleavy

In this short novel J. P. Donleavy writes of the tiny battle waged for survival of the spirit in bedrooms and hearts the world over. Samuel S, hero of lonely principles, holds out in his bereft lighthouse in Vienna. Abigail, an American college girl on the prowl in Europe, drawn by the beacon of this strange outpost, seeks in her own emancipation the seduction of Samuel S, the last of the world's solemn failures.

'Mr Donleavy manages to be funny about so much that one would have thought nobody could be funny about again – sole drunkenness, hangovers, American expatriates and tourists, and cross-talk from the psychiatric couch' – *The New Yorker*

A first-rate comedy of the saddest sort – *New York Times*

A haunting story, touchingly and outrageously told – *Boston Sunday Globe*

First published in the United States in 1966. To be published in England by Eyre & Spottiswoode and subsequently in Penguin.

Plays by J. P. Donleavy

The Ginger Man

Presented at the Fortune Theatre, London, in 1959.
Presented at The Orpheum Theatre, New York, in
1963.

Published with an introduction by the author,
What They Did in Dublin, an account of the play's
transfer to Dublin where it was made to close. In the
United States and in England in 1961.

Fairy Tales of New York

Presented at the Pembroke Theatre, Croydon, England,
in December 1960 and then transferred to the Comedy
Theatre, London, in January 1961. Winner of the
Evening Standard 'Most Promising Playwright of
the Year' Award in 1960.

Published in the United States and in England in 1961.
Available in Penguins.

A Singular Man

Presented at the Cambridge Arts Theatre, Cambridge,
England, in October 1964 and at the Comedy Theatre,
London, later that month.

Published in England in 1965.

a Penguin Book

A Singular Man

J. P. Donleavy

His giant mausoleum abuilding, George Smith, the mysterious man of money, lives in a world rampant with mischief, of chiselers and cheats. Having sidestepped slowly away down the little alleys of success he tiptoes through a luxurious, lonely life between a dictatorial Negress housekeeper and two secretaries, one of which, Sally Tomson, the gay wild and willing beauty, he falls in love with.

George Smith is such a man as Manhattan's subway millions have dreamed of being – *Time Magazine*

A masterpiece of writing about love – *National Observer*

. . . an utterly irresistible broth of a book – *Daily Telegraph*

First published in the United States in 1963 and England 1964.